Maurice Procter and The Murder Room

>>> This title is part of The Murder Room, our series dedicated to making available out-of-print or hard-to-find titles by classic crime writers.

Crime fiction has always held up a mirror to society. The Victorians were fascinated by sensational murder and the emerging science of detection; now we are obsessed with the forensic detail of violent death. And no other genre has so captivated and enthralled readers.

Vast troves of classic crime writing have for a long time been unavailable to all but the most dedicated frequenters of second-hand bookshops. The advent of digital publishing means that we are now able to bring you the backlists of a huge range of titles by classic and contemporary crime writers, some of which have been out of print for decades.

From the genteel amateur private eyes of the Golden Age and the femmes fatales of pulp fiction, to the morally ambiguous hard-boiled detectives of mid twentieth-century America and their descendants who walk our twenty-first century streets, The Murder Room has it all. **>>>**

The Murder Room
Where Criminal Minds Meet

themurderroom.com

Maurice Procter 1906–1973

Born in Nelson, Lancashire, Maurice Procter attended the local grammar school and ran away to join the army at the age of fifteen. In 1927 he joined the police in Yorkshire and served in the force for nineteen years before his writing was published and he was able to write full-time. He was credited with an ability to write exciting stories while using his experience to create authentic detail. His procedural novels are set in Granchester, a fictional 1950s Manchester, and he is best known for his series characters, Detective Superintendent Philip Hunter and DCI Harry Martineau. Throughout his career, Procter's novels increased in popularity in both the UK and the US, and in 1960 *Hell is a City* was made into a film starring Stanley Baker and Billie Whitelaw. Procter was married to Winifred, and they had one child, Noel.

Philip Hunter

The Chief Inspector's Statement (1951)
   aka *The Pennycross Murders*
I Will Speak Daggers (1956)
   aka *The Ripper*

Chief Inspector Martineau

Hell is a City (1954)
   aka *Somewhere in This City*
The Midnight Plumber (1957)
Man in Ambush (1958)
Killer at Large (1959)

Devil's Due (1960)
The Devil Was Handsome (1961)
A Body to Spare (1962)
Moonlight Flitting (1963)
    aka *The Graveyard Rolls*
Two Men in Twenty (1964)
Homicide Blonde (1965)
    aka *Death has a Shadow*
His Weight in Gold (1966)
Rogue Running (1966)
Exercise Hoodwink (1967)
Hideaway (1968)

Standalone Novels
Each Man's Destiny (1947)
No Proud Chivalry (1947)
The End of the Street (1949)
Hurry the Darkness (1952)
Rich is the Treasure (1952)
    aka *Diamond Wizard*
The Pub Crawler (1956)
Three at the Angel (1958)
The Spearhead Death (1960)
Devil in Moonlight (1962)
The Dog Man (1969)

Killer at Large

Maurice Procter

An Orion book

Copyright © Maurice Procter 1959

The right of Maurice Procter to be identified as the author of this work
has been asserted in accordance with the Copyright, Designs and Patents
Act 1988.

This edition published by
The Orion Publishing Group Ltd
Orion House
5 Upper St Martin's Lane
London WC2H 9EA

An Hachette UK company
A CIP catalogue record for this book is available from the British Library

ISBN 978 1 4719 0269 7

www.orionbooks.co.uk

1.

GUY Rainer's escape from prison was an action which followed closely upon an impulse; the chance was seen, and no sooner seen than taken. The alarm was sounded within minutes, but he was over the wall and away. In brown prison uniform he disappeared. He did this in a street thronged with people and traffic, because H.M. Prison of Granchester, better known as Farways Gaol, is surrounded by the city. The well-planned and oft-tried police cordon was formed, and it was thought that Rainer was trapped. But Granchester is a very big city, and therefore a very large trap. The subeditors of newspapers did not appear to regard it as any sort of a trap. "KILLER AT LARGE," their headlines yelled.

Detective Chief Inspector Martineau was inclined to agree with the newspapermen. "Rainer is a Granchester boy," he said. "He's at home here. He won't try to leave until he has somewhere to go and some safe means of getting there. And in the meantime he'll make himself hard to find."

"Don't you believe it," said Chief Superintendent Clay. He was head of the city's Criminal Investigation Department, and a man of even greater police experience than Martineau. "He can't remain at liberty in this town. He'll have to move out pretty quickly. Too many people know him. Also, in this town he is *local* news, and people are always more interested in local events."

"You mean there will be more people on the lookout for him

here? Possibly you're right. Do you think he'll try to get away by sea?"

"He was employed by a firm which did electrical work on ships, wasn't he? He's familiar with ships and it's quite likely that he'll try to get aboard one, either at this port or some other. Perhaps he'll have friends who might help him."

The two senior police officers were in Clay's office, and they had been busy over a map. Now Martineau rose to his feet. He was a tall, strongly built man, quite handsome in a rugged way, with a markedly blond head in which gray hairs could be seen if they were sought.

Clay remained where he was. His thick torso so exactly filled his office chair that he was reluctant to move when he had made himself comfortable. The hard little eyes in his big face seldom saw any humor in police work, but now he grinned.

"If we don't collar Rainer today, Mrs. Martineau is going to be very annoyed," he said.

The chief inspector nodded. The day was Friday. Payday. Fried fish day in the police canteen. The day before the week-end.

"Yes, it looks as if my week-end leave has gone for a burton," he said with a sigh.

It was Clay's turn to nod. He could perhaps have spared Martineau for the week-end, but he knew that Martineau would not spare himself. Guy Rainer was that officer's particular pigeon. It was he who had arrested Rainer and charged him with manslaughter.

"I sent him down," he said. "It's my job to see that he goes down again."

"How are you going to set about it?"

"Find out who his friends are, for a start-off. His case was such a straight up-and-down job there was no need to dig into his background. Result, we know very little about him. His parents won't tell me anything, but I can try and find his ex-sweetheart. She has no reason to love him, now. She might tell me who his friends are. Also, I'll go to the place where he used to work. I might get to know something there."

That was the end of the conference. Martineau went to his own office and sat down at his desk. He reached for the telephone and then sat in thought, with his right hand on the instrument. He turned up his left wrist, and looked at his watch. The time was now five minutes past five of a mild, dry April afternoon. All day he had been out of town, on a journey to Leeds to give evidence of arrest in the case of a lone-wolf post office raider. He had returned to his own "manor" expecting to have nothing more to do than draw his pay, make up his diary, and start that precious and long-awaited week-end leave. "He's done it on me," he mused with rueful humor. "The little blighter is getting some of his own back."

The man he would soon be seeking had made his escape late in the forenoon. He had got away and gone to earth at the busiest time of the day. How had he managed that? An assisted escape? That was not probable. He was an honest man who in a fury had killed another man, and he was not known to have criminal acquaintances. The prison authorities, who usually know such things, had said that he had not become friendly with any habitual lawbreakers while he was inside. So, presumably, without help he had remained at liberty in broad daylight for more than five hours. That was remarkable.

In less than three hours the daylight would be gone, and Guy Rainer would have the cover of the night. And in less than half an hour the place where Rainer had once been employed would be closing for the day, and perhaps for the week-end. Martineau remembered the name of the firm. He consulted the local telephone directory, and dialed a number. He spoke to the manager of the firm and made an appointment, then he rang for a car.

He went out into the main C.I.D. office, where Detective Sergeant Devery was waiting for him. The sergeant's smile of greeting was genuine. "Are we off now, sir?" he asked, as eager for the chase as a young foxhound.

3

Martineau nodded, and walked toward the main entrance. Devery matched his long stride with ease. He was equally tall, and ten years younger. He was also, in a manner of speaking, ten years more agile, and though not so heavily muscled as his companion he could still be described as a formidable man. On the very rare occasions when masculine beauty was the parade room topic, other policemen had to admit that Devery was a good-looking fellow, because their wives had told them so. The wives spoke freely on this matter because Devery was a bachelor, no woman's property and therefore a legitimate subject for speculative discussion.

A plain C.I.D. car was waiting outside the main entrance. "You drive," said Martineau to Devery. "Maracaybo Street, down by the docks."

The manager of the Moderna Marine Engineering Company could not answer Martineau's question, but he found a reluctant foreman who could. "Now Andrew," he said. "You've got to help the police in this matter. Rainer is a menace while he's at large. He'll be desperate. He'll trample on anybody who gets in his way."

"I realize that, Mr. Brady," said Andrew without enthusiasm. "I'll help if I can."

"How did Rainer get on with his mates when he worked here?" Martineau wanted to know.

"He got on all right. He was a bit moody, like, but he weren't a bad lad."

"Was he particularly friendly with any of them?"

Andrew hesitated, then he said: "Two of 'em were real pals of his. The three of 'em used to go about together. At nights, I mean, when they weren't working."

"Do those two work here now?"

"No, they both left."

"Why did they leave?"

4

"They left as fellers do sometimes. Thinking they might do better with another firm, happen."

"Did they leave together?"

"No. They went at different times."

"What are their names?"

"One is called David Barber. He's a tall, slim lad with light hair. He has light eyes too; blue or gray."

"Where does he live?"

"With his parents. His father keeps a pub somewhere in Burnside."

"What is the name of the other man?"

"Alan Clare."

"What's he like?"

"A medium sort of chap, well made. Just about the same size as Rainer, in fact. He has a darkish coloring and dark eyes."

"Where does he live?"

"He lives somewhere in Burnside an' all. Or at least he did do the last I heard."

"Thank you," said Martineau. "It would be better for everyone, including yourself, if you kept absolutely quiet about this interview. See what I mean?"

"Don't fret yourself about that," said Andrew with feeling. "I shall say nowt, at no time."

The manager nodded in dismissal, and the foreman went away. Martineau asked for the addresses of Barber and Clare, from the books. These were supplied. At the time of leaving the firm, Barber had been living at the Dog and Duck Inn, Jasmine Street, Burnside. Clare had been living in Carmarthen Street, Burnside.

After a further expression of thanks, the two detectives made their departure. "Well, that's a start at any rate," said Devery, as they walked out of the building.

"Yes," Martineau agreed. "Now we can have those two discreetly watched.. If Rainer tries to contact either of them, his name's McCoy." And as they got into the car he said: "Stop at a phone box."

Three minutes later he was passing on his information to Clay. The C.I.D. boss wrote down descriptions, and said: "Right, I'll see to it. What are you going to do now?"

"Parkhulme. The Grayson family."

"Very well. Keep in touch."

Devery did not need to be directed to the Grayson home. He knew the address, Thirlmere, 49 Avon Road, Parkhulme, Granchester. He also knew the house. A man called Herbert Shell had been killed there, by Guy Rainer, when all the family except Patricia Grayson were out. Devery could still remember seeing the body lying in its own blood on the front room carpet. He wondered if that memory still troubled the Graysons in their home.

Avon Road was a wide suburban bypass. On one side of it the land was only partly developed, on the other side it was lined by neat, modern, semidetached houses. Across the road from the Grayson home, a new building was under construction. A big sign bearing the name of a well-known make of petrol indicated that when work was completed the building would be a filling station. Work was finished for the day, and the site was deserted. Martineau looked at it speculatively as he got out of the car, and he turned to look at it again after he had pressed the bell button on the front door of No. 49.

Mrs. Grayson opened the door. She was a plump, middle-aged but still pretty woman with a face which showed her feelings as clearly as if she were putting them into words. When she saw the two policemen her face showed fear.

"Mr. Martineau!" she said. "What brings you? Has something happened? Is it Pat? Is it Dad?"

Martineau smiled. "Neither, as far as I know," he said. "You haven't seen an evening paper, then?"

She moved the door a little and looked behind it. "No, it's

here," she said. She stooped to pick up the paper. "What is there? What's happened?"

"Guy Rainer has got out of jail."

"Oh!" Her hand went to her mouth. The mouth was open in horrified surprise. "What will he do if he sees Pat?"

"Run away, probably. I wouldn't worry too much about Pat. That isn't the reason why I want to see her."

"She'll be home any minute. Will you come in? Dad is out too. Will he be all right? Would Guy hurt him?"

"He has no reason to," said Martineau, as he stepped hat in hand through the doorway. "You worry too much, Mrs. Grayson."

She went ahead of the two policemen, leaving Devery to close the door. "Sheila," she called as she entered the living room. "Guy Rainer has escaped!"

Martineau was on her heels. He saw the younger Grayson girl, whom he had not seen for four years. She was a handsome, fair-haired girl; a schoolteacher, he remembered. Now she would be twenty-two or twenty-three years of age, he thought. While he made that guess he watched her reaction to the news.

She put a hand to her throat. She lost color. That was natural, he supposed. But there was a sudden glint in her eyes which he could not quite understand. It looked almost like excitement or triumph. Then it faded, and was replaced by unmistakable dismay. He waited to hear what she would say.

"Oh, the fool!" she cried. "The utter, utter fool! Now he'll lose his remission and everything."

"Serve him right," said Mrs. Grayson. "Frightening everybody to death."

The girl made no reply to that. She appeared to have regained control of her feelings. And Mrs. Grayson, after her meaningless outburst, remembered the conventions of hospitality. "Do sit down," she said to the visitors. "Would you like a cup of tea?"

Martineau declined the offer of tea. He said: "I wonder if

either of you could give me some information about Rainer. I'm trying to find out who his friends were."

"We'll help if we can, won't we, Sheila?" said Mrs. Grayson.

Sheila smiled faintly, and remained silent. The silence was noticed. Martineau said: "He'll be caught sooner or later. For his own sake it had better be sooner."

"My word, yes," Mrs. Grayson agreed. "The sooner the better."

"Who *were* his friends?" Martineau persisted gently.

"Eeh, now then," said Mrs. Grayson, deep in thought. "There were two of them. The Three Musketeers Pat used to call them. She was a bit jealous, I think, the way girls are sometimes. She didn't want Guy to have friends. Now what did they call them, Sheila?"

"*I* don't know," said Sheila.

"Of course you do. One of them, his father kept a pub. Eeh, what was his name?"

Nobody mentioned the name. Martineau asked: "Were there any other friends, besides those two?"

"Not that I ever heard tell of, but Sheila will know."

"I *don't* know," said Sheila. "Guy was engaged to Pat, not me."

Mrs. Grayson stared at her daughter in surprise, but she did not argue against the blank denial. "Well," she said helplessly. "We'll just have to wait till Pat comes home. Are you sure you won't have a drink of tea, Mr. Martineau?"

"Since I'm waiting, a cup of tea would be very nice," the chief inspector said, and the good lady bustled away to the kitchen.

The tea had been drunk and a cigarette smoked before Patricia Grayson arrived. She entered breezily, slamming doors with careless vigor. She was a big, redheaded girl of startling attractions. Her vivid personality was shown by her every look and action. The sight of the two detectives rising to their feet kindled green fire in her eyes.

"Yes, I've heard," she said aggressively to Martineau. "I don't see that it's any reason for you to be here. Why the hell should we have to be dragged into everything?"

Martineau understood her perfectly. Once she had been a naughty girl. She might still be a naughty girl. Her unfaithfulness to Guy Rainer had led to a young man's death. She still lived in the street where that had happened, and she lived in defiant contempt of gossips. She held her head high. If she suffered, she did not show it.

"Take it easy," he said with a smile. "I'm just making a routine inquiry. Nobody is going to drag you into anything."

"I'll damn well make sure they don't. What do you want?"

"Rainer will have to get food, money and clothes. He might do that by robbery, or he might seek the help of friends."

"You don't think anybody in this house would help him, do you?"

"No. But you might help *me*. Who were his friends?"

"Alan Clare and David Barber."

"Any other close friends?"

"Not that I know of."

"H'm. He has no brother or sister, but what about other relations? Was he particularly fond of a cousin or an uncle?"

"No. They weren't that sort of a family. They didn't bother with relations. At least, Guy didn't."

"Thank you," said Martineau. He was silent for a moment, then he said: "This question may be a waste of time, but I must ask it. Was he friendly with any other girl? Is there any woman who might help him?"

"Only his mother," said Pat drily.

Martineau picked up his hat. "I don't think you'll be troubled again," he said, then he and Devery made their departure.

Outside, he looked again at the half-built filling station. "A man could watch the house from there," he said. "Let's have a look round."

The two men searched the building site, then returned to their car. "Telephone," said Martineau as he climbed in.

9

From the nearest public kiosk he again spoke to Clay. "The Grayson family told me what I knew already," he reported. "I think we ought to have a man watching the house."

"Never mind that now," said Clay unexpectedly. "I'm putting you on another job."

"But I was going over to Burnside to—"

"You're going to Burnside all right, but you can forget Guy Rainer. There's a nine-year-old girl missing. Her name is Desiree Kegan. Does that ring a bell?"

"No."

"Never mind, it will in a minute. Got your book handy? Right, here's the description. Desiree Kegan, nine years, medium size for age, plump but not fat, dark hair, brown eyes, rosy cheeks. Wearing blue school coat, tan beret, tan shoes and white socks. The address is 28 Mold Street, off Wales Road somewhere. A P.C. 942 Vincent got the complaint from the kid's mother. She's two hours overdue from school. The division has taken over the general search, but I'm putting you on to work independently until the child is found. You see, there are one or two funny angles to this. The parents don't live together, and the father wants custody and hasn't got it. He once actually snatched the child, and had to give her up. If he's snatched her again, our part of the job should be easy, but there's another side of the story which I don't like at all. Do you remember reading in the paper, a few weeks ago, about a little girl in Burnside winning a thousand pounds with a Premium Bond which somebody had bought her for her birthday?"

"I remember something about it," said Martineau.

"Well, Desiree Kegan is that girl. If the worst happens to her, she represents a thousand nicker to her next of kin, namely her parents. A thousand is a lot of money in Burnside. Anything might have happened. That's why I want you nosing into the job, whether the div likes it or not."

"Very good, sir. While I'm looking for the kid I can keep one eye and one ear cocked for Rainer."

"The primary job is the child," came the harsh dictum from the other end of the line.

"Yessir. Has the father been interviewed yet?"

"No. That's for you."

"I'd better see the father first, I think. Where does he live?"

2.

THE district of Burnside was roughly a mile square, and its innermost fringe was about a mile from the city's center. It was a place of mills, factories, foundries and engineering works. In residential terms it was called "working class," and most of its houses were small, and old without the attraction of antiquity. They stood in rows, all more or less alike; smoke-darkened, slate-roofed brick boxes, with tiny back yards and front doors opening straight onto the street. Burnside was not far from Granchester's inland port, and from some of its longer streets the masts and superstructures of big ships could be seen. Being near to the docks, it had a considerable colored population. Sikhs, Lascars, Levantines and Chinese were commonly seen in its byways, and there were also many Jamaican and Nigerian immigrants. Sometimes these people made work for the police, but they made not half so much work as the native Burnsiders, whose English blood was strongly laced with Irish and Welsh. English-Irish-Welsh can be a very potent mixture. In many parts of Burnside the policemen patrolled in pairs.

In Burnside also there were small neighborhoods and groups of streets which were "respectable." Martineau happened to be aware that in Mold Street, where Desiree Kegan lived, there were scrubbed doorsteps, clean windows and clean curtains, and the

11

inhabitants were not in the habit of fighting with either friends or strangers.

But seven or eight hundred yards of busy Wales Road had to be traversed between Mold Street and Collier Street, where Desiree's father now resided. At twenty minutes past six on that fine Friday evening Wales Road was thick with people and traffic. The two detectives rode along beside a curb thronged with women finishing the day's or the week-end's shopping, it being understood that this vital business included window gazing and gossiping in groups. The pubs and shops stood cheek by jowl as it were, their close opposing lines broken only in one place by a small public park. As Eden Street was approached there was a noticeable deterioration in the appearance of both the shops and the houses along the side streets. The roughest part of Burnside was on the right of the crossroads where Holly Road and Eden Street joined Wales Road. In short, Eden Street was the roughest part.

The two men went along Eden Street to Collier Street, where they saw dirty windows, dirty doorsteps and dirty curtains. The street was shrill with unwashed children. Thin mongrels and thinner cats slunk about. Smells emanated from open doorways. Slatternly women sat on doorsteps, and looked at the two obvious detectives with not unfriendly eyes.

Two middle-aged women sat together. They looked as if they had lived in Collier Street for a long time. Martineau spoke to them through the open window of the car. "John Kegan. Which is his house?"

One of the women moved her head. "Next door but one," she said.

"Have you seen him at all this afternoon?"

Both women shook their heads. This might have meant that they had not seen Kegan, or it might have meant that they refused to give any more information. Devery drove on to next door but one.

The door of the house was wide-open. There was no sound

from within. Martineau tapped on the door. "Come in, whoever you are," a man called. The two policemen entered the house.

From the front door they stepped straight into the living room. It was an untidy room. There was a big square table in the middle of it, and the tablecloth was a grease-spotted newspaper. The rest of the room's furniture—armchairs, settee, sideboard— was comparatively fine; cheap modern stuff only a few years old.

A man and a woman sat at the table, eating fish and chips. A year-old child sat on the thin hearthrug. Wearing nothing but a short singlet he was visibly of the male sex, and he was making his face greasy with a chip.

The man was of medium height and build. He was about thirty-five years of age, swarthy and handsome, but he had the fanatical look of a man with noisy and unshakable opinions. He looked strong and virile in his working clothes—soiled blue over-alls and an open-necked sweater.

The woman was ten years younger; palpably in her prime. She was dark-haired, as sleek as an otter. She had a brown-eyed stare and a mouth like a scarlet smear on a pale oval face, and there was no doubt that she had a shape. Young Devery's glance swung to hers like a needle to the north. He was slightly incredulous. She was wearing an old house dress, but he could easily imagine what she would look like when she was dressed to appear in public.

"Mr. Kegan?" Martineau asked. "John Kegan?"

"That's me," said the man: not hostile, but ready to be.

Martineau introduced himself and Devery. The man nodded. "I knew you were police," he said. "What do you want? I don't owe anything."

"On account of what?" Martineau queried. "We're not bailiffs."

"On account of maintenance money. I don't pay it any more. Not since my wife got herself a cock lodger."

"I'm not concerned with that. I'm making inquiries about your daughter Desiree. Have you seen her today?"

Kegan put down his knife and fork. He pushed back his chair and rose to his feet. The woman stared at him without expression. The child held out its mangled bit of greasy potato to him and made noises.

"Are you trying to tell me something's happened to Dessie?" he wanted to know.

"She hasn't arrived home from school," said Martineau.

Kegan turned pale, but he kept his emotions under control. "So you've come here for her, is that it?" he asked.

"Your wife seemed to think that she might be here."

"Not this time. The next time I take Dessie it'll be legal. I haven't seen her since Tuesday. Search the house if you don't believe me, but make it snappy. We've got to get cracking. We don't want to be fooling around in here while my kid is missing."

"Do you mind if we look upstairs?"

"No. Go on. Get on with it."

Martineau nodded to Devery, who began to make a quick search of the house. Kegan resumed his seat at the table. He picked up his knife and fork, then he put them down and pushed his plate away. He looked straight ahead with unfocused gaze.

"By God," he said somberly. "If Lucy has let any harm come to my kid, I'll throttle her."

John Kegan's idea of setting out in search of his daughter was to go straight to her home in Mold Street. "I'll begin there," he said. "I'll get to know the facts for a start off."

"You know the facts already," said Martineau, who suspected that the man intended to make trouble.

"You're the police, you'll do it your way. I'll do my way," was the stubborn reply.

The inspector reflected that if there were going to be a few home truths spoken, he might as well hear them. "I'll go with you," he said. "Just to see if there's anything new. We'll go on foot. The sergeant will bring the car."

During the ten-minute walk, Kegan talked. "I shoulda had my

little Dessie all along," he complained. "But my wife got the custody, on account of I'd left her and gone to live with another woman. I did snatch her once—if you can call it snatching a child what's willing to come with you—but the wife came with the police and I had to give her back."

"You said she was willing," Martineau interposed. "Do you think she would be willing to go anywhere with a stranger? Or someone she knew only slightly?"

"You mean be led away?" Kegan's frown of worry deepened. "I shouldn't think so. I hope not." He made a sudden, impatient gesture. "I shoulda had her. I'da looked after her a lot better. And I *will* have her, legal. I'm saving up to hire a barrister. Since Lucy took Sam Jolly to live with her, she has no more right to the kid than I have."

"Who is Sam Jolly?"

"He's a half-inch bookie. Oh, legitimate, I suppose. He has a bit of a wood hut with a telephone and a tape machine."

"No runners?"

"You'd better ask him. I'm no copper's nark."

Martineau reflected that a small-time bookmaker in that district would have difficulty in staying in business unless he employed runners to collect ready-money bets in factories and pubs, and on street corners. Probably most of the bets which Jolly took were illegal, but that did not matter. It was irrelevant to the job in hand.

"And this Sam Jolly actually lives with your wife, you say?" he asked.

"He reckons to be only a lodger. Ha! There's only two bedrooms. You can't tell me he don't sleep with her."

"How long has he lived there?"

"A twelvemonth, happen."

"And how long since you left your wife?"

"Four year."

So, the policeman thought, Mrs. Kegan had lived a grass widow's life for three years before she had taken a "lodger." It would hardly be comfortable living, with a child to support and little enough money coming from her husband. Perhaps she had waited three years for him to return. According to the standards of Burnside, that was too long for any woman to wait. Her neighbors would not blame her for taking another man. But why hadn't she got a divorce? Probably she had let the matter slide until she became friendly with Jolly, and that was that. Some people had the damnedest, slapdash, haphazard way of living.

"Is Jolly married to somebody?" he asked.

"Yes. Parted from his wife. No kids, though."

Martineau nodded. It was just as he had thought. What a carry-on!

"Have you lived in Collier Street for four years, then?" he asked.

Kegan looked up at him. "What's this, my life history you're wanting?"

"Just background. You're Dessie's father, you know."

"Let's find the kid first, and then write the biography."

"I'm saving time by getting it now. What is the name of the girl you live with?"

"Rosa. Rosa Vizard."

"Is she married too?"

"Yes. Her husband's a dead loss. He's been in the loony bin."

"Really!" Martineau was interested. "Was he certified?"

"No, persuaded. Voluntary patient."

"Who persuaded him? His wife?"

"How do I know?" Kegan snarled. "His doctor, I suppose."

"Were you friendly with his wife at the time?"

"Well, I knew her."

"Did that worry him?"

"I don't know what his worries were."

"H'm. Have you lived with Mrs. Vizard the whole four years since you left your wife?"

"Yes."

"So the baby on the hearthrug is hers and yours?"

"Yes."

"Any other children?"

"No."

"Where did Mrs. Vizard live before she went to live with you?"

"Same place as she lives now."

"I see. You moved in with her. Was that while her husband was in the mental home?"

"Yes," was the reluctant answer.

"My word, I'll bet that did him a lot of good."

"It didn't do him no harm. He got better, didn't he? He's out now. Been out two or three years."

"Was there any trouble when he came out and found you living with his wife?"

"Trouble? With that whippersnapper? I could break him up for firewood."

"Where is he living now?"

"What's that got to do with anything?"

"I'm asking you."

Kegan scowled, then stopped as an idea struck him. "Do you think that little drip could have hurt Dessie? To get his own back on me?"

Martineau shook his head. "You said it, I didn't. Do you think he's a man who would do that?"

"A man who's been in the hatch is liable to do owt. You should know that."

It was not much of an answer, but Martineau let it go. "What is Vizard's full name?"

"Albert. If he has a middle name I never heard of it. If he's hurt a hair of my kiddie's head, I'll paralyze him."

"Where does he live?"

"With his sister, in Flint Street."

Martineau nodded. He knew where Flint Street was. He had by no means finished with Kegan, but he let the man go the rest of the way without further questioning. He did not yet want to

17

mention the matter of Dessie's thousand pounds. That could be discussed later, when he had more knowledge of the people with whom he was dealing.

When they reached Mold Street, where Devery was already waiting beside the car, Kegan led the way to the open door of his wife's home. He would have walked into the house without knocking if Martineau had not put out a hand to stop him. Martineau knocked, and the woman he guessed to be Lucy Kegan was at the door in an instant.

She was perhaps thirty years of age, neither pretty nor plain, with a small, neat figure, brown hair and blue eyes. Her hair, while not dressed in the height of fashion, was glossy and well kept. The dress she wore was ordinary but becoming. Her eyes were puffy and reddened, and when she saw that the knock on the door did not mean that her child was being restored to her, it seemed that her tears would start again.

Martineau announced his rank and name. "You are Mrs. Kegan?" he asked.

She nodded, but she was looking at her husband. The question in her glance was met by an accusing glare.

"Did he have her?" she wanted to know.

"Apparently not," Martineau said.

"Oh, dear!" The tears came. She turned and ran back into the house. Her estranged husband's face did not soften in sympathy. The hard, intolerant scowl remained.

Martineau stepped into the doorway. "May we come in?" he called.

"Sure, come in," came the answer in a deep masculine voice.

The three men entered. The room was moderately well furnished, and it had the usual square table in the middle. The table was bare except for a spotless white cloth, which may have been laid in preparation for tea before Dessie became overdue from school. Lucy Kegan now sat at the table, with her elbows upon it and her face covered by her hands. In an armchair near the hearth, facing the window, sat a short, plump, thin-faced, sallow man, with sleek black hair and a wisp of black mustache. A cigarette hung so naturally from a corner of his mouth that it looked as if it might have grown there.

"Good evening," this man said, without rising. "Find yourself a chair. She'll be able to talk to you in a minute."

The two policemen sat down. Kegan remained standing. "*You've* found yourself a chair, at any rate," he said to the sallow man with dislike.

"I know when I'm well off. You never did," the man replied calmly. He gazed up without fear at Kegan.

"Does *she* know she's well off?" Kegan gibed.

"Sure she does. She's better off now than she was when you were around."

"Oh, don't start a row," the woman said suddenly, sitting up and drying her eyes. "We have enough trouble."

Neither of the men appeared to have heard her. They were watching each other. Kegan was tense. He seemed to be angry enough to swing into action. The other man merely shifted his cigarette with an imperceptible movement of his lips. Now the cigarette was cocked upward at a subtly insolent angle, and a small cloud of smoke was blown toward Kegan.

"Stop it, I tell you!" the overwrought woman cried in sudden anger, and Kegan turned to her.

"Why didn't you go to meet Dessie from school?" he demanded. "That's what you shoulda done every day."

"Steady," said Martineau. "Easy now."

But the woman was answering her husband. "Don't you try to make out our Dessie hasn't been looked after," she said with spirit. "She had strict instructions to come home every day with Mary Hartley and Annie Steele."

"And did she keep to those instructions?"

"She hasn't been doing, lately. But I didn't know."

"There you are, you see. She needs a father's care. If I'd been looking after her she'da done as she was told."

Lucy Kegan sniffed. "That's what you say."

19

"When Dessie is found," Kegan said deliberately, "*I'm* going to take care of her."

"You're not going to do anything of the kind," the man in the armchair said with perfect equanimity.

"I'll go to court. I'll get her legally."

"I'll fight you with my last penny. That woman of yours isn't fit to look after a child."

"Keep her name out of it!"

The man in the chair did not raise his voice. "All right," he said. "We'll make that easy. You get out of this house, then your tender feelings won't be hurt. You've no business here. You aren't helping to find Dessie by coming here and shouting the odds."

"You can't order me out. This is Lucy's house."

"This is *my* house. I took it over and bought it as a sitting tenant. Now get out."

"I want to know where that child is," Kegan persisted.

"Well, you won't find out by standing there and arguing. You're only distressing Lucy. Go on, scarper. Before I ask these officers to throw you out."

Kegan looked at Martineau in appeal. The detective was expressionless. "I'll see you later," he said.

"I'll do you for this, Jolly. I'll get my own back," yelled Kegan, obviously burning with rage and humiliation. He turned and plunged blindly through the doorway. When he had gone there was a brief silence.

"Sorry, gentlemen," said the man in the chair. "I can't stand the big-headed no-good. He only wanted to hurt Lucy."

"You're Sam Jolly?" Martineau asked.

"That's me. And I can't abear a welsher."

"Is Kegan a welsher?"

"He welshed on his wife, didn't he? Went off with a slut. He hates his wife because he knows he didn't do right by her, and he hates me because he knows she's happier with me than she was with him."

"Was he lured away by Mrs. Vizard, or did he do the luring?"

"About fifty-fifty, I should say. She's a sly bitch. Ignorant as hell, but cunning."

"She's what they call a smasher," Martineau probed. "Very attractive."

"Oh, aye, I daresay," Jolly agreed without interest. Lucy Kegan looked down at her clasped hands on the table.

Martineau addressed himself to her. "I gather that you've been talking to Dessie's playmates," he said. "Why didn't she come home from school with them?"

"She waited for the teacher. It turns out she's been doing that for a week or two. I didn't know. Nobody told me."

"Does the teacher live somewhere around here?"

"No. She lives out at Parkhulme. But it seems Dessie has been in the habit of walking with her as far as her bus stop in Wales Road, then coming along home alone. Happen the teacher didn't see anything wrong in that, but oh, I wish I'd known."

"If Dessie came part of the way home with the teacher today, that's very important," said Martineau, rising to his feet. "We must look into that. What is her name?"

"Miss Grayson, they call her."

"Grayson? Parkhulme? Not Sheila Grayson!"

"I don't know her first name."

Martineau described Sheila Grayson. "Yes, that sounds like her," Mrs. Kegan said.

"Do you happen to have a telephone?"

Jolly answered. "No," he said. "I don't do any business here, you see. The nearest phone will be at the Flying Dutchman, just at the top of Mitchell Street. The first place you see when you get to Wales Road."

For that information thanks were given, and the two policemen departed. At the Flying Dutchman Inn they found a pay telephone. "When we can find the time," Martineau grumbled as he searched among his change for pennies, "we'll turn that boneshaker in and get ourselves a radio car."

"Anything new, sir?" he asked when Clay came on the line.

"Nothing new," was the gruff reply. "We're all busy here, getting nowhere. The father didn't have the child, then?"

"Apparently not. Not in the house, anyway."

"Have you seen the mother?"

"Yes. And the fellow who lives with her. I haven't scratched the surface there, yet, because the mother set me off on a new lead. Dessie Kegan has been in the habit of walking part of the way home with her teacher. I'll have to talk to the teacher. Also, there's another character I must see. His name is Albert Vizard. He's been in a mental home, and he has a sort of motive. While he was inside, Kegan took his place in the happy home, and stayed there."

"Yes, you'll have to see him. Want any help?"

Martineau did not want help, but he pointed out that he could get on with his business better if he had a radio car. Clay promised to send one to his next calling place, which was Parkhulme again.

It was dark when Martineau and Devery arrived at the Grayson house for the second time. This time the doorbell was answered less promptly. Mrs. Grayson could be heard, asking nervously: "Who is there?"

Martineau answered: "Police," and gave his name.

"Are you sure?" the good lady wanted to know, and then Patricia interrupted with an impatient "Oh, mother!" and flung open the door.

She stood on the doorstep barring the way. If a beautiful girl could be said to scowl, she scowled. "You're soon back," she snapped. "You said we wouldn't be bothered again."

"So I did," the chief inspector replied crisply. But I haven't come to see you this time. I'm not in pursuit of Guy Rainer, either. I must see your sister. One of her pupils, a little girl, hasn't got home from school yet, and nobody knows where she is."

"Oh, dear, the poor little thing," said Mrs. Grayson.

But there was no womanly concern on the face of Patricia as she stood aside for the policemen to enter. Her expression was thoughtful and speculative.

"Do you think Guy could have had something to do with that?" she asked.

3.

ONCE more seated in the living room of the Grayson home, Martineau noticed the change in Sheila's manner when the matter of Dessie Kegan was mentioned. The cloak of cold reserve was discarded, and the true nature of the girl was revealed. She was instantly worried about the child, and anxious to give all the information she could. She answered the detective's questions intelligently, as might have been expected of a member of what is possibly the most important profession in the world.

"Yes," she said. "Dessie has made a habit of waiting for me during the last few weeks. It does happen occasionally that a little girl gets a pash for a teacher. I usually humor them until they get a pash for something or somebody else."

"Was she waiting for you today?"

"Yes, but I sent her home. I had an errand. She wanted to come with me, but I wouldn't let her. I wish I had, now."

"What time was this?"

"Not later than five minutes past four. I got away in good time today."

"Did you see Dessie go on her way?"

"Yes. I watched her go skipping off along Holly Road, then I turned in the other direction."

"Did you see anyone speak to her, or approach her in any way?"

"No."

"That was the last you saw of her?"

"Yes."

"Would you mind if I asked you what was your errand?"

"Not at all. A child called Agnes Brown is away from school with some sort of gland trouble. Her mother wrote and asked me to call and see her. That was my errand."

"What was the address?"

"Twenty-seven Sedan Street. I got it out of the register."

"Was there no address on the letter?"

"No."

"Have you still got the letter?"

Sheila looked around. "I believe I still have it in my bag."

"Here's your bag, dear," said Mrs. Grayson.

Sheila found the letter in the bag and passed it to Martineau. He looked at the small cheap envelope and the postmark. The address, penciled in shaky block letters, was: "MISS GRAYSON, TEACHER, BURNSIDE JUNIOR SCHOOL, GRANCHESTER."

He found a single sheet of inferior paper in the envelope. He read the letter:

DEAR MISS GRAYSON,

AGNES IS ABOUT THE SAME BUT SHE FRETS A LOT MISSING SCHOOL. SHE TALKS ABOUT YOU A LOT COULD YOU CALL AND SEE HER. I WOULD ESTEEM IT A PRIVELIGE.   YRS SINCERELY,   MRS. BROWN.

"Do you mind if I keep this?" he asked.

"No," said Sheila. "But why?"

"There's no address and the whole thing, even the signature, is in block letters. You saw Mrs. Brown, I presume. Was the letter mentioned?"

"No, I don't believe it was."

"What did she say when she opened the door to you?"

"I remember quite well. She said: 'Why, Miss Grayson! How nice of you to call! Do come in. Agnes *will* be pleased.' "

"H'm," said Martineau. "How long did you stay?"

"About an hour. Mrs. Brown made me a cup of tea."

"Then you came straight home?"

"Yes."

"*Was* Agnes about the same?"

"Her mother said she was a bit better today."

Martineau slipped the letter into his pocket. He turned and spoke to Patricia: "Is there anything in the character of Guy Rainer to make you think he could have had something to do with this?"

"On second thought, no," the girl said.

"I should think not," said Sheila sharply. "That's ridiculous."

Patricia stared. "What's got into you?"

"Nothing," the younger sister said.

Martineau rose to his feet. "I won't take up any more of your time," he said.

Outside the house, a police mechanic was waiting to make an exchange of cars. Martineau relaxed gratefully in the roomier seat of the new car. "Drive to Sedan Street," he said, "and think of the days when we would have had to walk it."

At 27 Sedan Street, Mrs. Brown was quite positive in her assertion that never in her life had she written a letter to Miss Grayson. "And if I had," she said, "I wouldn't sign it as if I was filling in a football coupon. I just thought that Miss Grayson had called to see Agnes out of the kindness of her heart."

Martineau thanked her and returned to the car. "Now we'll go and see Mr. Albert Vizard," he said. "And on the way I'll report progress."

The Vizard house in Flint Street was an architectural replica of the Jolly-Kegan establishment in Mold Street. Its doorstep was equally clean, and furthermore it had a doorbell which was in working order.

25

The doorbell was answered by a buxom, red-faced woman who seemed to be about forty years of age. Most of her was covered by a flowered pinafore. She exuded energy and good health and, apparently, good cheer. She smiled at Martineau and Devery. They might have been friends who were very welcome.

"You'll be the police," she said. "Come in."

Her tightly girdled figure waddled ahead of them into the house. The room they entered smelled of furniture polish, and everything shone.

"Sit you down," she said hospitably. And when they were seated she went to the foot of the stairs. "Albert!" she called. "Some gentlemen to see you."

"He's having a lie-down," she said as she returned. "He'll be with us in a minute."

"Isn't he well?" Martineau asked politely.

"It's his depression," she replied without hesitation. "It comes and goes. Nothing you can put your finger on, like."

"He's been depressed today?"

"Yers. So he didn't go to his work. He sat in the park most of the day, I think."

"Don't his employers mind?"

"Oh, they mind all right. They want him there. But they understand. I reckon they have to. When he frames to go to work he's too good a man to sack."

"What does he do?"

"He's a cutter, a tailor's cutter, and one of the best. If it weren't for his depression he'd be making good money in a business of his own, instead of working in a sweatshop in Wales Road."

"When did his trouble start?"

"Four or five years since. It were his wife, Rosa. Just when he'd got the furniture paid for, an' all. She used to steal his money and spend it, and then she started bothering wi' Jack Kegan. He suspected her, but he weren't sure, and it used to worry him. He weren't too strong to start with, you understand.

And always a bit moody. So eventually he went to the 'sylum for a while."

"Was he a voluntary patient?"

"Oh, yes, voluntary. But because he's been in the 'sylum I knew as soon as I heard about little Dessie that you'd be round to see him. You needn't have bothered, really. He wouldn't hurt a fly."

"Has he ever tried to hurt himself?"

"Well, yes, once or twice. Nowt serious. Swallowing aspirins, and that sort of thing."

"Has he ever tried to hurt you?"

"Oh, no," the woman said quickly. A little too quickly, Martineau thought.

"You've never had any trouble of that sort at all?" he persisted, and as he did so he wondered if Albert Vizard was at that moment listening from the head of the stairs.

"None at all," she answered. "He knows I'm not afraid of him. He's not big enough to frighten me."

But if he were big enough, what then? Martineau wondered. But he said: "Who is his doctor?"

"Dr. Kennedy, in Holly Road," came the answer.

Martineau saw Devery make a note of the name. He asked a few more questions about Albert Vizard's general history, attainments, etc. Then he glanced at the woman's left hand. "Are you *Miss* Vizard?" he wanted to know.

Her merry laugh attempted to cover some embarrassment. Evidently she was one of those spinsters who are ashamed to be unmarried. "Aye, but I haven't give up," she said. "I'll have me a man before I've done."

Martineau grinned. "I'll bet you will. A man should be glad of a fine woman like you."

She loved that. Her eyes shone. "It isn't often anybody says owt nice to me," she said. "You're married, aren't you?"

"Yes. I'm married."

"I thought so. All the best is married."

"What is your full name, Miss Vizard?"

"Bertha Vizard. Big Bertha, some of 'em at the mill calls me. But not when they think I can hear 'em."

"I'll bet you can hit like a hammer. You'll scare all the fellows away if you talk like that."

"Not I," she retorted, enjoying herself. "Not a right man. I'm a woman for a right man. Same as a policeman, happen."

There were slow, heavy footsteps on the stairs; the footsteps of an infirm or weary man.

"You mun be careful with him. He's not quite himself," Miss Vizard said quickly in a low voice, and then Albert arrived. He was about thirty years of age, small, thin and pale, with a ravaged face. He was wearing a very good gray suit, but his shirt and tie were sloppy.

"Hello," he said casually to the visitors, as he made for an easy chair and slumped into it. "Phew! Do I look as lousy as I feel?"

"What's troubling you?" Martineau asked.

"Nothing. That's it. There *is* nothing. No excitement, no fun, no interest in anything."

"Why don't you go to the pictures, love?" asked Bertha maternally.

"Pictures, bah! Success stories and howling musicals."

"Well, why don't you read a nice book? You like to read."

"Not any more. I'm fed up with reading. And don't be saying there's something on the telly. That's the worst of the lot."

"Do you get much exercise?" Martineau asked.

"I've walked round Burnside Park a million times today. I thought you were a copper."

"I am."

"Then talk like one, not like a damned doctor."

Martineau was not noted for his patience with gratuitously insolent people, whatever their ailments were. "All right, I'll talk like one," he said grimly. "There is a nine-year-old girl by the name of Dessie Kegan who is missing from her home in Mold Street. Do you know the child?"

"I know her by sight. I've seen her with her mother."

"Does the child know you?"

"I don't know."

"Have you ever spoken to her?"

"I don't believe I ever have."

"Say yes or no."

"All right, NO! I'm not in the habit of talking to kids, especially little girls. It's dangerous for a man like me who's been in a mental hospital. People get ideas if they see you."

"Have you seen the girl today?"

"No."

"Would you like to give me an account of your movements from three o'clock this afternoon?"

"I'll give you my entire day. I was awake at half-past six this morning, when Bertha got up. I heard her getting the breakfast ready. She went to work. My alarm went at half-past eight, but I stayed in bed and let it run out. I couldn't have faced a suit length today for all the tea in Ceylon. I dozed till nine o'clock and got up feeling as brown as an old shoe. I took a pill, but it didn't make me feel any better. There were cornflakes and a bacon sandwich for my breakfast. I took one mouthful of cornflakes and then threw them into a corner, plate and all. I expect Bertha cleared it up, and you'll find the broken plate in the bin."

Martineau looked at Bertha, and she nodded guiltily.

Albert went on: "I had a bath, and felt no better. I came to the conclusion that it's impossible to drown yourself in a bath. The water gets up your nose and you have to come up to sneeze. I had a shave, but you can't cut your throat with an electric razor. Oh, we have everything here, believe me. My sister looks after me as if I were her one lonely chick."

"I can see that. Go on."

"I stared out of the window for half an hour, thinking about pleasant ways of dying, then I put the morning paper in my pocket and went out into the sunshine. I sat on a seat in the park. It was a grand morning, but the birds were making a nerve-racking din. I started to read the paper, and it was full of the most depressing stuff. Murders; some silly little twirp sounding off about the Duke of Edinburgh; bureaucratic tyranny; trouble in the Middle East; somebody twisting the lion's tail again; imports up and exports down. I couldn't care less. I—could—not—care—less. To hell with everybody."

"Do you smoke?" asked Martineau curiously.

"I never smoked. Silly habit."

"Do you take a drink?"

"Oh, mister! Don't mention it! If I drink when I'm taking my pills I'm a sick, barmy wreck in no time at all."

"I see. Hard lines. How long did you stay in the park?"

"Till half-past twelve or so. Some kids came in there on the way from school. I could gladly have murdered two or three of 'em, but I didn't."

"Why could you have murdered them?"

"Because of the damned noise and helter-skelter they were making."

"Was Dessie Kegan one of those kids?"

"I don't think so. I've already told you that I haven't seen her today."

"So you have. I'd forgotten. So you left the park at half-past twelve and . . . ?"

"I came home, and had a cup of tea and one cold bacon sandwich. I lay on the sofa and tried to go to sleep, but it was no good. I got up and took another pill and went out. I was feeling just a bit better. I went into the park again and walked about till I was tired. Then I sat on a bench right up in the top corner. I had it to myself, nice and quiet. That was all right. I sat there till the sun went behind a cloud and I felt just a little bit chilly. I got up and came home then."

"What time was that?"

"I couldn't tell you exactly. Happen about a quarter past four."

"Did you see anyone you knew?"

"In the park? One or two old regulars I know by sight. Nobody to speak to."

"Did you see anybody you knew on your way home?"

"No."

Bertha intervened, with surprise in her voice. "Didn't you go for your money, Albert?"

Albert's glance flicked to Bertha, then returned to Martineau. "Oh, yes," he said. "I forgot. After I came out of the park I went to the shop for my money."

"Where is the shop?"

"In Wales Road. Thomas Horner and Company. Number five hundred and forty-one."

"Whereabouts in Wales Road is that?"

"Right on past Holly Lodge. About three hundred yards past. It was hardly worth going for. Only two days' money this week."

"What time were you at the shop?"

"Half-past four, maybe."

"Which way did you come home from there?"

"Straight on Wales Road, of course."

"So you walked past the end of Holly Road. Did you see anyone you knew?"

"No," said Albert.

"When you got home, did you go out again?"

"No. My sister can prove that. She was home soon after five."

Martineau absent-mindedly lit a cigarette, then he said: "Have you been wearing that suit all day?"

Again Albert's glance shifted momentarily toward Bertha. "No," he said. "I've changed since I came home."

Further questions were answered to the effect that Albert had also changed his shoes and tie, but not his socks and his shirt. Martineau looked at Bertha. She was listening quite placidly. Apparently the answers were true.

"Do you mind if I look at the things you were wearing today?" the inspector asked.

"Why do you want to look at them?" Albert wanted to know. But Bertha said: "What does it matter? I'll get them."

She went upstairs, and returned with a blue suit, a pair of black shoes and a red and blue tie. Martineau and Devery took them to the window and examined them. They did not find any bloodstains or other suspicious marks.

"I think you've got a nerve," said Albert, when the examination was over.

"Routine," said Martineau curtly. He looked at Devery. Devery put away his pen and slipped his notebook into his pocket. The two policemen said good night, and departed.

They drove from Flint Street into Mitchell Street, and along Mitchell Street toward Wales Road. "Well, Dr. Devery," said Martineau, "what is your medical opinion of Albert Vizard?"

"If he didn't look so ill I'd say he was just spoiled and lazy," the sergeant answered. "As it is, I don't know."

"He doesn't ring true to me. That business about the bath and the electric razor was a lot of clever-clever talk. He's conceited. But I'll admit he does look ill."

"He swings on that sister of his."

"He sure does. She's worth ten of him. You'll notice he didn't apologize for slinging his breakfast and breaking a plate. Obviously he hadn't mentioned it to her before."

"There's one thing that stands out like the nose on your face."

"Say 'sir' when you speak to me. I know what you mean. Without being asked he gave us the full story of his entire day. As far as we can tell, he mentioned everything that happened. Everything except the one thing that mattered. Do you suppose he could really have forgotten that he walked nearly the full length of Wales Road just about the time when Dessie Kegan should have been coming from school?"

"I don't believe that for a minute. He was trying to conceal the fact."

"And that makes him a suspect," said Martineau. "I'll put out the word on him. We might get to know a little more about what he did between four and five this afternoon."

They came to the junction of Mitchell Street and Wales Road. "What now, sir?" asked Devery.

Martineau looked across the road, at the little inn from which he had telephoned earlier. "I'm thirsty," he said. "Let's have a pint at the Flying Dutchman."

The barmaid at the Flying Dutchman was a dark-eyed, lively lass. A bouncer, Devery mentally classified her. Not a bouncer to throw 'em out, but a bouncer to bring 'em in. Nevertheless, her bar was not busy so early in the evening.

"Do you want to use the phone again?" she asked.

"Not this time," said Martineau. "We want two pints of your very best bitter beer."

The girl bent her dimpled elbow in the business of drawing beer. "Is it true?" she asked. "There's a little girl missing from around here?"

"It's only too true, I'm afraid."

"Oh, dear! What's her name?"

"Kegan. Dessie Kegan."

"Not Jack Kegan's little girl!"

"John Kegan is her father, yes. Do you know him?"

"Sure, I know Jack and Rosa both."

"Does he come in here?"

"Friday nights, Saturdays and Sundays. This was his local when he lived down the street with his wife, you see."

"Rosa wasn't around then, I suppose."

"Yes, she was. She used to come in here with her husband. Then she started coming in on her own, getting thick with Jack. Course she worked at the same place as Jack. Markham's Mill."

"Is that the mill at the end of Eden Street?"

"Yes. Across the road from Holly Lodge."

"Albert Vizard would be able to keep an eye on them while they were here, but not when they were at the mill, eh?"

"Albert couldn't do anything anyway. He was too little and weak."

"You see a lot of what goes on, don't you?"

"Yes, but it's none of my business so long as folk behave while they're in here."

"Fair enough," said Martineau. He drank the last of his beer. The barmaid picked up the glass and looked a question. "No. No more," he said. "We just wanted a thirst quencher."

The two policemen returned to their car. "We'll go and see Dr. Kennedy," said Martineau.

He lowered the side window as Devery put the car into gear. As it sped along he looked out at Wales Road, brilliantly lit by glowing yellow sodium lamps on high standards. Now, people and traffic were sparse. Daylight long gone, he reflected, and a man and a girl still to be found. No week-end leave for Chief Inspector Martineau.

At the crossroads made by the junction of Holly Road and Eden Street with Wales Road, Devery stopped behind a bus which was going in the same direction as himself. When the bus went burbling along Holly Road he remained in the rear of it, because he would soon have to stop at Dr. Kennedy's house. But the bus stopped again, just beyond the gates of Holly Lodge. The police car stopped behind it. Martineau glanced casually at the small group of people who had been waiting for the bus, and then he stared. Slinking past the group, who had eyes only for the bus, was a young man in a blue boiler suit and no coat. Martineau knew the young man. Rainer was the name, he believed. Guy Rainer.

4.

RAINER had seen Martineau, and had rec-
ognized him. He ran, going behind the car as the policeman
scrambled out of it. He crossed the road and ran straight to the
wall of the Holly Lodge grounds. He leaped at the wall, pulled
himself up, and scrambled over just as Martineau in headlong
pursuit grabbed for him.

Over the wall went Martineau after Rainer, but not with the
same agility. Devery, almost as agile as Rainer, overtook his
colleague and was over the wall before him. He had not seen
Rainer's face, but he did not need to ask questions. On the other
side of the wall he dropped into a tangle of shrubby growth and
deadwood. He stood still for a moment, and heard someone making crackling, swishing, rustling progress away from him. He set
off in pursuit as Martineau landed with a crash of breaking twigs
beside him.

The totally neglected shrubbery was like a jungle. Ancient
rhododendrons spread low and wide, making low caverns of
darkness where their branches touched the ground. Self-seeded
sycamores rose up in the gloom. Cypresses were cones of black-
ness. Everywhere were roots, brambles and deadwood to trip the
feet, and briers to clutch at garments and tear unguarded hands
and faces. Verdure and solid wood reduced visibility. Silent
movement in the tangle was impossible. Devery crashed on after
Rainer. A whipping branch took away his hat, and he let it go.
The honor of making this capture would be worth twenty hats
to him.

Martineau did not follow the sergeant. He stumbled along the
side of the wall until he reached the wide, padlocked iron gates.
From the gateway he could run in silence on the grass beside the

drive. Moving thus on the edge of the trees he realized that now there was only one man crashing forward in there. Rainer had emerged, or else he was lying low.

The drive curved away toward the big house, which had been unoccupied for more than twenty years. It took Martineau further and further away from Devery's course through the shrubbery. But about a hundred and fifty yards up the drive there was a path which joined it at an acute angle. This path through the shrubbery was bordered and roofed in by two rows of beech trees, and was very nearly in complete darkness. Martineau stood and peered along it, but could see no movement. He stepped aside and concealed himself behind a big tree.

Now there was silence among the shrubs. Martineau waited. In a little while he heard a rustling approach. Presently he saw that it was Devery, walking on the path's thick carpet of rotted leaves. He showed himself, and the sergeant came to him.

"He hasn't come this way, then?" was the immediate whispered question.

"I doubt it," Martineau replied. "I would have seen him. He may be hiding somewhere in there, or he may have got to the side wall and gone over."

"It *was* Rainer, of course?"

"It was Rainer, all right. Now, you leave me here and go back to the car and get on the air. I want a tight cordon around this place. Also you can report that Rainer is now wearing a blue boiler suit, no hat, no coat. It might be a good idea to show some light and make plenty of noise near the wall before you go over."

"Very good, sir." Devery's voice was regretful as he turned to walk down the drive. The fugitive who had been such a short distance ahead of him would now probably be arrested by some other police officer.

Martineau remained where he was, listening. He heard Devery moving about near the wall, and then there was silence in the grounds of Holly Lodge. It was in his mind that if Rainer was hiding in the grounds he would guess that one of his pursuers had gone to make a call for more men. Rainer would see that as an obvious move. Therefore he would soon make a move himself.

Rainer moved. He moved so carefully that only one small snap of breaking deadwood informed Martineau of his position. Martineau began to walk as silently as possible along the path. When he heard the swishing of sapling branches he knew that his man was near. He stood still then, scarcely breathing. When he perceived that the man was going to break cover a few yards further along the path he stepped aside and stood behind the nearest beech tree.

Martineau's eyes had grown used to the darkness, but he heard rather than saw the escaped convict emerge onto the path. He peeped round the tree, straining his eyes. He heard the rustling approach, and discerned a dark moving figure. When it was almost within reach, he pounced.

Rainer may have been surprised, but he was not taken by surprise. Martineau, possibly the most formidable man in the eleven-hundred-strong Granchester City Police, was the one who was taken by surprise. In his experience the boldest of men had always recoiled, momentarily at least, from a sudden attack in the dark. But this man did not recoil. He stepped forward and thrust like a swordsman, and for a brief moment Martineau thought that he had run into the end of a broken branch. The hard jab in the stomach stopped him and doubled him up, then a blow to the head sent him down like a smitten ox.

He was up on one knee for a count of eight, and soon thereafter he tottered to his feet. But there was no opponent to knock him down again. Guy Rainer was away, out of sight and hearing.

Martineau's body was full of pain, and the entire left side of his jaw was sore. He felt it tenderly, and decided that it was not broken. He realized that he had been hit with something cold, hard and heavy; an iron bar or a poker, or something of that sort. Rainer, apparently, was a natural counterpuncher. His instinct was to meet an assailant halfway, and the fencer's lunge with his piece of metal had been the most effective thing he could have done. As his anger cooled, the thwarted policeman perceived that he could have been even more unfortunate. Rainer was a hotheaded killer. Instead of swiping Martineau across the jaw he could just as easily have cracked his skull.

Martineau followed the path to its end, which was a little glade among the trees. In the middle of the glade there was an old stone seat, and the remains of an ornamental fountain. The glade was quite near to the side wall of the Holly Lodge grounds. He thought that Rainer might have gone that way, over the wall.

He walked back along the path, and set off down the drive. He met Devery.

"They're on their way," the sergeant said. "Horse, foot and artillery. They're going to surround this place."

"They'll have to cast the net a bit wider, I think," said Martineau.

Devery peered. "What's the matter?"

"I met him. Nearly got my hands on him. He took a poke at me with an iron bar."

"Oh, dear. I'll get a car. Shall it be home or hospital?"

"Headquarters," said Martineau. "I'll work sitting down for an hour or two."

A section sergeant from Burnside marked Martineau's map for him. "All these here are condemned houses," he said, busy with his pencil. "Empty. No windows or doors, and plenty of dark cellars. There's bombed-out ground here, here and here. St. Mary's is here, and churchyard. Burnside Methodist here, and churchyard. This here is a mill dam, and it's deep. Kids have been drowned there. Here's the abattoir. Nobody would notice a bloodstain or two there. Here's Burnside Park. Not very big, but plenty of cover. Here's Markham's Mill, with plenty of stuff dumped in the mill yard. Empty weft boxes and such. This factory here is empty. The firm who's got it don't seem to need it yet. Here's the school. And here's Holly Lodge. It belongs to the

City Corporation now, but they don't seem to know what to do with it. The garden is a wilderness."

"Don't I know it," said Martineau. "Proceed, Sergeant."

There were other places; factories, foundries, laundries, dye works, garages, a brewery, Burnside Chemicals, Burnside Plastics, Burnside this and Burnside that. Many of them were closed until Monday morning, but they would all have to be searched long before then. The superintendent of the division was already using every man he could get, including special constables, and managers and caretakers were being notified of the necessity to search. Though the people of the neighborhood had not yet started to help, at nine o'clock that night, by word of mouth alone, almost everyone living within a mile of Dessie Kegan's home knew that she was missing.

The coincidence of her disappearance only a few hours after the escape of a convicted killer from a nearby prison loomed large in the public mind. It made the affair into a sensation; pie for the press. Local journalists had sent their pieces off to Fleet Street, and the national papers were already sending their top reporters to Granchester.

Having acquired a sound general idea of what the rest of the force was doing, Martineau folded his map and went along to Clay's office.

"Hello," said the C.I.D. chief, in a tone which suggested that the explanation would have to be convincing. "What's this I hear? Is it true that you let Rainer give you the slip?"

"I let him give me more than that," said Martineau, and he told the story briefly.

"Hard luck," was Clay's comment. "So he's got himself some sort of a club. I'll put the word out on that. How did you get on with Vizard?"

"If there has been a crime against the child, Vizard is definitely a possible client. And I think there has been a crime. Read this letter."

Clay took the letter and read it, and then Martineau told him of his inquiries in connection with it. The superintendent's expression grew more somber as he listened.

"There may be fingerprints on this," he said. "I'll keep it and let Sergeant Bird have a go at it in the morning."

"Prints *might* come in handy, if ever we make an arrest."

"I don't like this at all. I felt trouble in my bones as soon as I heard the kid was missing. That's why I wanted you on the job from the start, nosing around as if we already had a crime. But I'll admit I never dreamed that we'd have a teacher decoyed away and a child deliberately waylaid. If that is what happened, it's ten to one we've got a murder on our hands."

"And a damned nasty one, too. There's one thing. If the note does have a connection with the child's disappearance, then Guy Rainer couldn't have had anything to do with it."

"No. I never thought much of that angle, anyway."

"The fact that the teacher was got out of the way suggests that somebody wanted to intercept Dessie between the school and the teacher's bus stop. This somebody didn't want to contact Dessie after she had passed the bus stop. Therefore he had some particular place in mind."

"Yes. Holly Lodge is the best bet."

"The gates are locked."

"Not in the daytime. Some Corporation men have been working at the house all week, replacing rotten floor boards."

"The grounds were searched in daylight, I suppose?"

"Yes. It was the first place I thought of. And now we've got men searching all around there in the dark, looking for Rainer."

"What about dogs?"

"We tried them. They were no more good than they were when we tried to pick up Rainer's trail this morning. It must be the variety of city smells, or the hard pavements, or something."

"Too bad," said Martineau. He touched his jaw, and found that it was swollen.

"Are you still feeling shaky?" Clay asked. "Got a headache or anything?"

"I'm all right, sir. A small pain in the guts and a sore jaw, that's all."

"Well, there isn't a right lot more you can do tonight. Why don't you go home and sleep it off. Then you'll be ready for work in the morning."

"I'll stay on the job a bit longer, if you don't mind."

"All right. But not later than eleven o'clock unless there's something doing. That's an order."

"Very well, sir. Eleven o'clock," said Martineau. His supper would still be warm when he got home, he knew. Because of Guy Rainer's escape from Farways, his wife Julia would not be expecting him home before that time.

Before eleven o'clock the report came in. There was no sign of either Guy Rainer or Dessie Kegan in the Holly Lodge area. Following the report came a bundle of statements taken by detective officers. Every known "queer fellow" in Granchester had been interviewed. Every man with a record of offenses against children had been closely questioned. Seedy migrants in hostels and common lodging houses had been "turned up." Martineau volunteered to help Clay with the work of perusing the documents.

"No," said the superintendent firmly, though he was undoubtedly tired. "I shall want to read them all myself, anyway. You go home."

Martineau went. When he got home he found his wife waiting for him and his supper ready to be served, as he had expected. He told her the news. Ever since the early days of their marriage he had confided details of his work to her. She was the soul of discretion: his career was hers.

Womanlike, she was concerned about the missing child. "The agony the poor mother must be suffering," she said.

"The father wasn't exactly overjoyed about it, either," said Martineau.

He tried to imagine what his own feelings would be if the missing child were his small daughter Susan. He wouldn't be able to bear it, he supposed. In a way, he sympathized with John Kegan. He certainly understood why the man had behaved as he had. He guessed that in similar circumstances he too would want to blame somebody.

"All the same," he decided, "I shall have to have further words with Kegan. It's too early to eliminate him entirely."

He thought about Kegan. During his career he had encountered many convincing actors who had never walked the boards. Kegan could be putting on an act. Suppose that he had, after all, tried to get little Dessie to leave her mother and go to him. And suppose Dessie had refused, and in his disappointment, jealousy and injured vanity he had struck the child. Suppose he had struck her too hard. A blow of the fist of a man like Kegan might easily break the neck of a nine-year-old girl.

5.

MISS Sheila Grayson had no practical reason for going to Burnside School on Saturday morning. She had told the police all that she knew about Dessie Kegan, and if they wanted her again before Monday they would look for her at her own home.

But she could not sit at home and endure the company of her mother. Mrs. Grayson was a nice woman who normally had nothing on her mind but gossip and ordinary domestic affairs, but now she was obsessed with irrational fears about Guy Rainer. Mrs. Grayson said, not once but twenty times, that she would die if Rainer's face appeared at the window. Sheila also thought about Rainer, with feelings of half-guilty excitement. Yesterday the police had hunted for him in the grounds of Holly Lodge, and Holly Lodge adjoined the school.

Though nobody had blamed her in any way, Sheila also felt that she was partly to blame in the matter of Dessie Kegan. She wanted to be once more assured, by some person other than her mother, that she was blameless. So she went to the school. She was sure there would be somebody at the school who would want to talk the matter over. In view of what had happened, Mr. Kenworthy, the headmaster, would almost certainly be there.

Mr. Kenworthy was not there. None of the staff was there. Not even Hardacre, the school caretaker, was there. He lived a little distance away and apparently saw no reason why he should be at the school on Saturday morning after the police had searched it on Friday.

Sheila had a key for the main door, which was at the front. But she walked round the outside of the building, undecided about entering, savoring her disappointment, and feeling quite lonely. On Saturday morning the place seemed so much different. The heel taps of her smart shoes echoed in the schoolyard. She was more accustomed to the echoing voices of boisterous children.

Still, though she decided not to enter the school, she did not go away immediately. She returned to the front of the building and waited, thinking that someone might come. In any case she had to wait for her sister. Patricia had gone shopping in town, in the secondhand two-seater MG which she had bought with her saved-up earnings as a typist. She had promised to drive round by the school on her way home and pick up Sheila.

Sheila had waited for less time than a minute when she was joined by a young constable whom she had seen several times before in that district. Apparently he also had walked round the building, because he came round the corner near the front door as she had done. She did not hear his approach, but saw him as soon as he appeared. He looked tired, but he was shaven and clean. His buttons reflected the morning sunshine, his trousers were pressed, and his boots had a military gloss.

"Good morning," he said with a smile. "Waiting for some-one?"

"I teach here," she said. "I thought the headmaster might be here this morning."

"Does he usually come on Saturday mornings?"

"No. But there's a little girl missing, one of my class. I suppose you know all about it."

"I know something about it. I wish I knew more. I got the report, you see. It's my job, in a manner of speaking. You'll be Miss Grayson, then?"

"Yes. I wondered if I would be needed here this morning."

"There's nobody showed up at all, yet," he said, thus inform-ing her, perhaps unintentionally, that the school was under surveillance.

She thought that he was nice, and nice-looking. He was straight and strong, and of course respectable. It occurred to her that she had heard of quite several teachers getting married to policemen. It was just a thought, the sort of thought that a young girl may have.

"I suppose it was silly of me to come," she said.

"Oh, I don't know," he replied. "I'd say it was a reasonable thing to do, in the circumstances."

"Do you just walk round and round the building?"

"This building and others. I saw you arrive and go round the back, so I trailed after you."

"To see what I was up to?"

"To see that you didn't come to any harm."

"What harm could come to me in a schoolyard?"

"The same harm that could come anywhere else. There's a bad man loose in this area."

"Did you expect him to attack me?"

"I did not. But if he had done, I'd have been Johnny-on-the-spot."

"And that would have been a feather in your cap, wouldn't it?"

"I suppose so. If I could have nailed him. But as I told you, I'm chiefly interested in the other job, the little girl."

"Do you think something—something awful has happened to her?"

P.C. 942 Vincent did think so, but he said: "We mustn't jump to conclusions. She might be all right."

Then he proved that while he might appear to be committing the disciplinary offense of Idling And Gossiping While On Duty, he was wide-awake and watchful. "Press!" he said suddenly. "Do you want your picture in the paper?"

"Oh, no!" she answered in a distressed whisper. "No!"

"Then turn your back, quickly," he urged. "Get away from here."

Men were getting out of a taxi which had stopped at the gate. She turned. The key of the school door was in her pocket. In a moment she was at the door, the key in her hand. She opened the door and stepped inside, and closed the door without turning to face any camera which might be focused upon her. She locked the door.

Outside, Vincent stood stolidly while a cameraman took photographs of the school and himself at the door. There was also a reporter, who approached.

"Morning, Officer," the reporter said breezily. "Who was that who just nipped into the school?"

"One of the staff."

"Which one?"

"I couldn't say."

"Was it Dessie Kegan's teacher?"

"You know very well I'm not allowed to give *any* information to the press. If you want to know anything, you'll have to go higher up the line."

"This is the school, isn't it?" the reporter queried, not without sarcasm.

"This is Burnside Junior School."

"You speak very well, for an ordinary constable."

"You don't do so badly yourself, for an ordinary reporter."

The newspaperman laughed, and on the other side of the strong oaken door Sheila heard the laughter faintly. She turned away and passed through an inner door, and then she stopped, appalled by the noise of her own footsteps, and by the grim, deserted corridor. Burnside Junior was not one of your modern glass-and-concrete schools. It was at least seventy years old; a sound building of soot-blackened brick; two-story for the most part; clean, well maintained and rather gloomy. Ahead of her stretched the main corridor, floored with maple blocks and illuminated through one big window at the end, and through the glass doors of classrooms. The quietness and comparative gloom oppressed her, but she went forward, her high heels clicking bravely on the maple.

It was with a feeling of relief that she put her hand on the door of her classroom. Through the door she could see that it was flooded with sunlight. Also, it was her own familiar room. She could not feel unreasonably nervous in there.

She entered, and she was closing the door behind her when she saw something which gave her nerves a sickening jolt. A man was standing near the door, with his back pressed against the wall. He stepped forward and closed the door, and even when she had recognized him she was some time in recovering from her shock.

He had been tense, ready to pounce. But when he saw that she was not going to scream he relaxed. "Hello, Sheila," he said. "You teach at this school, don't you? I'd forgotten."

She looked at Guy Rainer. He was wearing an old boiler suit over prison clothes, black unpolished boots and a belt. She recognized the belt as one which had been in her desk.

"That's my belt," she said.

He nodded. "I found it in the desk there. I borrowed a penknife as well."

"Borrowed?"

"I needed a belt and a knife. Someday I'll replace them."

"Now that you know they're mine, and I know you've got them."

"Oh, call it stealing if you like. I'm on the run. All the world is against me, and I can't afford to stick at trifles."

"Am I against you, then?"

"You're the one who knows that. Are you going to turn me in?"

"Of course not," she said.

They stood, considering each other. He needed a shave. He was much paler than he used to be, and perhaps a few pounds lighter in weight. But the real difference was in his expression. His face was set in bitter lines. He looked as if he had never laughed and never would. And his voice was different. He talked quietly and flatly, without inflection. It was a manner of speaking which suggested ruthlessness. Here was a man who spoke when he had to, and meant what he said, no matter how outrageous it might be.

"You've grown into a very handsome woman, Sheila," he said. "I chose the wrong sister." The words were not compliments; they were statements of fact.

So, she thought, he had realized it at last. She had been the truer and better of the sisters, and perhaps, now, the better-looking. But that had been five years ago. He had regarded her as a mere child, and anyway he had had no eyes for any girl except her sister. Sheila had thought that he was wonderful, and she would have been his for the asking. Why had she felt like that? she pondered now. There had been nothing outstanding about him. She wondered if her feeling for him would return, and if so, when.

"You don't bear any malice, do you?" he wanted to know.

"Why should I?" she retorted. "You didn't hurt anybody of mine."

That was true. It was "the other man" he had killed. Patricia Grayson had made the mistake of not breaking off her engagement before she took a lover. Perhaps she had never intended to break off the engagement. Then quite by accident Guy had caught the two together, on a still summer afternoon when there had been nobody else in the house. There had been a steel poker within reach. Guy had killed the man. He had not laid a finger on the girl. In those circumstances if the girl had been his wife he would have been sentenced to a short spell of imprisonment, or none at all. But because the girl had not been his wife but his fiancée, the judge had taken a different view of the matter. Guy had been put away for seven years. With remission for good conduct, that had really meant a term of just over five years. He had served nearly four years, and escaped.

Sheila had known. She had hated her sister for being untrue to Guy, and she had longed fiercely to tell him. But she had said nothing to him, though she had warned her sister that he would eventually find out for himself. He had done so, with what dreadful consequences.

"How is Pat?" he asked.

"She's all right. Does that matter to you?"

"Not a bit. I never want to see her again."

Womanlike, she was tempted to goad him. "I bet Pat could still twist you around her little finger," she said.

His expression did not even change. "Not a chance," he replied.

"Why did you do it?" she asked in sudden anger.

"Do what? Kill Bert Shell?"

"No. Why did you escape? With your remission you had only just over a year to do."

"It's hard to explain," he said. "I'm not going to try."

He assumed that he would never be able to make her understand. Some men in prison could settle down and count the days with equanimity if not contentment. Others were like trapped beasts. Guy was one of the latter sort. He was a man who had always liked to be out of doors, moving around, and prison had been punishment indeed. He had tried to be patient and philosophical. Another three years . . . Another two years . . . Only another eighteen months . . . But when he had seen the opportunity to escape he had slipped away without a second thought, like a leopard slipping from a broken cage. The wild exultation of those first moments of freedom had died away now, but he still refused to regret his escape. He was out, and he was going to stay out as long as he could.

"You"ll never have a minute's peace," she said.

"At least I can see the stars at night."

"Why don't you give up, and go back? Walk out of this place with me."

"No. They'll have to catch me."

"There's a policeman outside."

"I know. I've been watching him."

"Why not go out to him?"

"No."

"This may be more serious for you than you think. You got out of prison yesterday. A few hours later a little girl was missed. She hasn't been found yet. You know what people are. They're blaming you."

"Could I have something to do with it? I mean, does she live around here?"

"She goes to this school, and she lives not far away. Dessie Kegan is the name."

"I don't know her. Is she any relation to Jack Kegan?"

"His daughter."

"Too bad. I'm sorry about that. Do *you* think I've done something to the kid?"

"No. And I have a reason for believing that the police don't think so, either. But everybody else is connecting you with the child."

He was watching her narrowly, suddenly suspicious. "How do *you* know what the police think?" he demanded.

"They've been to see me. Dessie was one of my class. So far as we know, I was the last person to see her."

He relaxed. "Oh," he said.

49

"You can't survive. Everybody will be after you. And if a mob gets hold of you it may be very bad."

He was impassively thoughtful. Then he said: "I'll just have to be more careful, that's all. If only I could get hold of some money . . ."

Involuntarily her fingers tightened on her handbag. "*I* won't give you any money," she said. "I won't tell the police about you, but I refuse to help you. You're being foolish. If you would surrender voluntarily to the police it might not be so bad for you."

He remembered his encounter with Martineau in the grounds of Holly Lodge. A faint, tough grin appeared momentarily on his face. There was one policeman who would be thirsting for his blood, at any rate.

"How did you get in here, anyway?" she wanted to know.

The grin reappeared. "I used to go to school here, didn't I? I was a nosy little beggar. I know the place inside out."

"Were you in this building when the police searched it?"

He shook his head. "I'm not telling you anything, Sheila," he said. "The less you know about me, the better for yourself."

"That's true, I suppose," she admitted. And then she said: "I'd better go. If the policeman has a key he might come in here to tell me that the reporters have gone."

He was tense again. "What reporters? Are *they* ferreting around?"

She allowed herself a touch of sarcasm. "Of course they are. You're a famous man now, didn't you know? You're on the front page of every newspaper in the country."

"On account of the kid?"

"I think that will have a lot to do with it."

He regarded her narrowly. "Why did you come in here?" he questioned, with sudden harshness.

"I told you. To escape the reporters."

"Why did you come to the school at all this morning?"

She was liking him less and less, and becoming afraid of him. "I came to see if anyone was here," she said.

"Who, for instance?"

"Mr. Kenworthy, the headmaster."

"Why? Why did you want to see him?"

"Well, one of my children is missing. I thought he might want to know more about it."

"H'm." He was silent, watching her. For some reason he had become as distrustful as a wild animal.

A door banged. The brisk tapping of feminine heels could be heard coming along the corridor. Sheila knew that walk. It was her sister, come to take her home.

In his prison boots Guy tiptoed away from the door. He motioned to Sheila to move away also. She shook her head, and remained where she was. She saw anger and panic blaze in his eyes as he looked around for cover. There was no cover. The furnishings of the classroom were small desks and a blackboard, and cupboards too small for him to hide behind. Even the door would not hide him, because its glass panels were not heavily frosted.

Patricia walked quickly. "Where are you, Sheila?" she called, and of course she came straight to the classroom.

Sheila did not see Guy's hand move to the rule pocket of his boiler suit, but she saw the short crowbar which he brought out. "Stand aside," he grated. He assumed that the newcomer certainly would tell the police about him, immediately and at the top of her voice. But if he could get hold of her and put the fear of death into her she might be induced to keep quiet long enough for him to get away.

"Stand aside," he repeated.

Sheila was wide-eyed with fear, but she did not move. Guy stepped forward and thrust her aside. She dropped her handbag and caught his left arm with both hands. "Let go, damn you," he muttered furiously.

Then Patricia arrived. "The policeman let me in," she said cheerfully as she opened the door. Then she saw Guy, and the iron bar.

"Keep quiet and don't move," he snapped.

But she was away, flying down the corridor on wings of fear, running like a boy. Guy started after her, but Sheila held on to his arm.

"No," she panted. "No. Don't hurt her." She clung to his arm with frantic strength.

"Let me go, you treacherous bitch," he bellowed, beside himself. He raised the crowbar and brought it down on her head. She moved her head to avoid it, but received a glancing blow which felled her. He did not look at her as she dropped to the floor, but ran out into the corridor. He saw that Patricia had reached the front door. He turned and ran the other way.

6.

"THERE now. Feeling better?" the young doctor asked.

Sheila murmured an affirmative reply, and gave him back the glass. Even though her head ached, she felt much, much better because she was safe and because Patricia appeared to have come to no harm. She glanced up at three solicitous, down-looking faces, Devery, P.C. Vincent and a sergeant in uniform, and at three impassive ones, the doctor, Patricia and Martineau. She smiled. She smiled wanly. The others returned the smile with varying degrees of warmth.

"We won't need an ambulance," the doctor said. "You'll be all right. Rest and quiet will do the trick."

"I'll take her home, Doctor," said Patricia.

The doctor nodded, closed his bag, said good day and departed.

52

"Before you go, just give us the picture," said Martineau. "It *was* Guy Rainer, I suppose?"

"Yes," Sheila replied, almost in a whisper.

"Did he hit you with something?"

"Yes. An iron bar. But I don't think he meant to hurt me. He was in a panic because I was holding on to him."

"Were you trying to prevent him from getting hold of your sister?"

"Yes."

"Had he threatened you at all, before that?"

"No. I had been trying to persuade him to give himself up."

"Do you think he will?"

"He said he never would. You haven't caught him, then?"

"No. He dodged us again," said Martineau. He continued to ask questions, and this time Sheila gave him his answers. He learned how Rainer had refused to tell her about his movements or his plans, and how she had refused to help him with money; how she had tried to show him that his position was hopeless, and how he had appeared to become distrustful of her.

"Would you have told the police about him?" Martineau asked.

"I had said I wouldn't. That's why I didn't call out to Pat when she came. It would have made him think that I was trying to betray him."

"But you held him long enough for her to get away. You did well there."

"He called me a—he called me treacherous. I think he believed I was trying to hold him until Pat brought the police."

"And actually you were only concerned with Pat's safety?"

"That was it, more or less," Sheila replied. Strangely enough, she did not feel unhappy about what Guy thought of her. She had been honest enough with him, and he ought to have trusted her. She had only prevented him from hurting Pat, and probably getting himself into worse trouble than he was in already. What did he think he could have done? Killed them both to ensure silence? They had only needed to scream, and he would have been lost. He could have done nothing, and he had not had the sense to see it. She felt a spark of anger against him when she remembered what he had called her.

"I'd like to go home," she said.

"But of course," said Martineau. He was by no means convinced that the girl had told him the whole truth, but at the moment there was nothing else he could say to her.

Sheila rose to her feet and swayed. He caught her arm and steadied her. Patricia moved up on the other side and said: "I'll take her."

Sheila disengaged herself from both of them. "I can manage, thank you," she said coldly. She walked unaided out of the classroom and along the school corridor. Patricia walked beside her, but did not touch her. Sisters they might be, but they were not physically close.

When they were in the little open car, Patricia turned down the windshield. "We'll let the fresh air blow on your face," she said. "You look as if you need it."

"What about you?" Sheila queried. "It must have been a shock."

"Oh, no," said the elder sister savagely. "I'm a real heroine, I am. I run like hell and I care not what happeneth to thee, Jack."

"It was the only thing you could do. It made Guy run away."

"After he'd bashed you with a piece of iron."

"Well, that wasn't so bad. What happened when you got outside?"

"I ran to the bobby yelling about Guy Rainer being inside. He was in there like a shot. When I followed him in, he was pounding about from classroom to classroom. I followed him into your classroom and saw him having a look at your head. He said to me: 'Find some smelling salts, if you can,' and then he went galloping off into the basement. He was back in a minute, gabbling into that pay telephone in the corridor. I did a Lady of the

Lamp act with the salts out of the ambulance box. Then in no time at all the place was full of policemen."

"How did you feel about betraying Guy to the police?"

"Betraying hell!" Patricia snarled. The little car came to a sudden stop behind a car which had stopped even more suddenly, without warning, at the junction of Holly Road and Wales Road. Patricia's horn blared angrily. She followed the offender into Wales Road, then contemptuously overtook him and spurned him with her dust.

"Betraying!" she repeated in disgust. "That idiot? He was never anything but grief to me."

"Well, you did let him down," said Sheila with spirit.

"Whose side are you on? So I was having a bit of fun. I wasn't married to him, was I? He could have settled the matter like somebody right in the head, instead of going stark, staring barmy and killing somebody, and dragging us all in the mud with him. Betraying! Don't give me that! The sooner he's back in jail the better he'll be."

"Well, you knew he was hot-tempered and jealous."

The glorious red head turned, and the green-eyed glance swung to Sheila's face. "What sort of sentimental claptrap is this? What's the matter with you? You sound as if you're in love with the crazy fool."

"Well, I'm not," said Sheila. "Watch your driving."

No further word was spoken until they were home, where the news had to be given to Mrs. Grayson. That lady showed as much alarm as she was capable of showing. She would not be convinced that Sheila's meeting with Guy had been quite accidental. She was sure that he had been lying in wait for her daughter.

"This is terrible," she said. "He'll never forgive us on account of Pat. He might murder us all. We'll all have to stay indoors till he's caught."

Her daughters did not argue with her. Sheila was not going out, anyway, and Patricia would certainly go out when she wished. They warmed to each other enough to exchange a smile when their mother went to make sure that the doors were locked.

Meanwhile, in Holly Road, Martineau heard the report that the school and the district around it had again been unsuccessfully searched. There was not a trace of either Rainer or Dessie Kegan. More policemen were moved into Burnside. Plain-clothes men in pairs were now given small areas to search thoroughly and patrol constantly, while other men were stationed at crossroads and similar vantage points, to watch the passers-by. It seemed that it would be impossible for either Rainer or Dessie Kegan to remain undiscovered.

In Martineau's mind, as in the minds of his superiors, the Dessie Kegan case had priority. It was imperative that the mystery of the child's disappearance should be solved. As time went by his feeling that murder had been committed became stronger. But, if there had been a murder, where was the body? Everything possible had been or was being done to find the child alive or dead. Or, Martineau corrected himself, *it was thought* that everything possible was being done. He tried to bear in mind the possibility that more might be done, and that ideas of what this extra form of action might be could come through the business of eliciting information. The Dessie Kegan case was like any other. It was a matter of search, inquiry and observation.

He had by no means finished his interrogations of the Kegan-Vizard and Jolly-Kegan families. Also, Albert Vizard was a large question mark in his mind. Also, he would have to talk to Sheila Grayson again, but perhaps more with regard to the matter of Guy Rainer than of Dessie Kegan.

Another thing was the letter which Sheila Grayson had received. If it had any significance—and it seemed to have—it served the double purpose of indicating a premeditated crime and of narrowing the circle of suspects for that crime. If the letter was not a hoax it pointed to a number of facts. Somebody had known that Miss Grayson was beloved of her pupils and was a good sort. The same person had also known that a child called

Agnes Brown was ill, though he or she may not have known the child's address, because there had been no sender's address on the letter. The letter had been signed "Mrs. Brown," so it was probable that the one who wrote it did not know the Christian name of the sick child's mother. But the writer *had* known of Dessie Kegan's habit of waiting for her teacher after school, and walking part of the way home with her.

Martineau realized, with irritation, that it might not be easy to discover the identity of the unknown letter writer. In the first place the knowledge of Miss Grayson's popularity and Agnes Brown's sickness could have been acquired very easily by listening to the gossip of mothers at a shop counter, or in a bus queue, or on a park bench. The knowledge that Dessie Kegan regularly walked after school with Miss Grayson could have been gained by observation, while lying in wait for Dessie. The information that the teacher who walked with Dessie was indeed Miss Grayson could have been obtained by asking any child who happened to be passing when Miss Grayson was in sight.

"It's a sickening setup," said the chief inspector in disgust, as he and Devery walked along Holly Road, away from Burnside School. Then he said: "Here's Dr. Kennedy's place. We'll call and see if he has come back from his morning rounds."

They were in luck. The doctor had not completed his round of morning visits, but he had called at home for something he had forgotten. He was a good-natured, rather pompous, elderly man; not a terribly efficient practitioner, but well known and well liked in Burnside. He admitted that he had time to be briefly interviewed by the police, and then he began to ask questions about the two local sensations. Martineau humored this tacit implication that because he was the local doctor, he was not one of the common herd, and therefore had a right to know what was going on. He told the doctor as much as it was wise to tell, and then he steered the conversation round to the matter of Albert Vizard.

"Do you suspect Vizard?" Kennedy demanded.

"The word 'suspect' is too strong," said Martineau. "There is a connection. The child's father is living with his wife. What can you tell us about him, Doctor?"

Kennedy frowned. "There is a question of ethics," he said.

"Your ethics are safe with me, Doctor. Tell me what you can, without betraying your patient's confidence."

Kennedy cleared his throat. He put his hands behind his back. He paced about. He talked. The two policemen listened.

The doctor made some general remarks about nerves. Then he went on to say that the human brain, which human beings complacently accepted as a wonder of the world, was the most faulty and unreliable organ which nature had ever allowed to develop. He also commented upon the difficulties of medicine when there were few signs to give guidance. The listeners received the impression that there certainly was something wrong with Albert Vizard, but that Dr. Kennedy did not know what it was.

"Do you think that voluntary inertia could have something to do with his trouble?" Martineau asked.

"Laziness? Possibly. Many of them coddle themselves, and make out that they're worse than they really are."

"What about homicidal tendencies?"

"No evidence," said Kennedy promptly. Then, unwilling to commit himself even on that point, he said: "But you never can be sure."

Martineau rose and thanked the doctor. Then he and Devery departed. Outside the house he said: "I wonder how Kennedy would get on with the old coroner on the rampage."

Devery grinned. "He'd probably spill a lot more than he has done this morning," he said.

"He couldn't spill less," the chief inspector rejoined.

They passed Holly Lodge and came to Wales Road. A policeman in uniform was watching the pedestrian crossings at the road junction. Two plain-clothes men were watching the pedestrians. Across Wales Road, opposite the side wall of Holly Lodge,

Markham's Mill stood in its walled yard. Beside the factory Eden Street stretched away into the hazy, sunlit distance.

"While we're here, we'll go and have another word with Kegan," said Martineau. "Yesterday I had no chance to talk to him properly."

The time was ten minutes after noon. In Collier Street the children were playing noisily, and the women were sunning themselves on their doorsteps. A dairyman was delivering milk. He was near the end of his round, and somewhat tired. He was trying to fulfill his orders, collect payment, and at the same time keep an eye on the wolfish boys who, in their games, ran past his little truck and playfully swerved within snatching distance of the array of bottles.

"Perishing kids," he grumbled to the two detectives as they passed. "They'll pinch your bloody bootlaces."

As on the previous day, the door of the Kegan-Vizard house stood wide-open. Martineau tapped on the door. Kegan came to the door. He was spruce and clean, wearing what was probably his best suit. "Any news?" he asked.

"No, I'm afraid not," said Martineau. "I'd like to ask you a few more questions. May we come in?"

"Come in if you like, but I don't know what good you'll do. I gave you all the information I had, which was damn all."

"We have to keep asking questions," said Martineau as he stepped into the house. "Until we've asked, how do we know that you or Mrs. Vizard aren't in possession of some little item of information which might help us?"

Kegan grunted, and resumed his seat by the hearth. Rosa Vizard sat facing him across the hearth. The baby played at their feet. The two detectives remained standing.

"Where do you work?" Martineau began, though he already knew the answer to the question.

"Markham's Mill."

"Oh, yes, the mill on the corner of Eden Street. What do you do there?"

"I'm a sweeper."

"Do you mean a loom sweeper? Is it a cotton mill?"

"Correct."

The policeman reflected that the mill was directly on Dessie Kegan's route from school. It was also a point from which that part of the route could be watched.

"Were you at work yesterday afternoon, between four and five?" he asked.

"No, I wasn't," came the rather surprising answer. "I stopped work at four. I was in this house by two minutes past."

"Why did you stop work at four?"

"The mill always stops at four on a Friday. A lot of the weavers are married women. As soon as they get paid they want to go and do their shopping. So as a concession to them the whole shoot stops at four."

"I see. After you got home, how long did you stay in the house?"

"Till you came here, to tell me about Dessie."

Martineau looked at Rosa. "Were you at home?" he asked.

She nodded. "It's true what he says. I was with him the whole time."

"Except when you went to the shop," said Kegan.

"Oh, yes. He stayed with the baby while I went round the corner to get some fish and chips for the tea."

"What time would that be?"

"About quarter past five, happen."

Martineau thought that the girl had looked none too sure of herself when she answered, and he resolved to check the time of her errand. If she spoke the truth, it was unlikely that she had had any hand in the disappearance of Dessie. He thought about motive. She could be lying in support of Kegan. Submission to his wishes could be considered a motive. Or could she have a motive quite independent of Kegan's: a totally opposite motive, a desire to hurt the child or get rid of her? She might be jealous of Kegan's possessive love for Dessie. She might have wicked-stepmother feelings about her.

Considering this, Martineau decided that Rosa could not have any such motive. They were not living under the same roof, and normally they did not meet. Dessie was no nuisance to Rosa, and never had been. The fierce antipathy which could be engendered by Dessie's presence in Rosa's home and at Rosa's table could not yet exist. It could exist in the future, if Kegan succeeded in his plan to gain custody of the child, but it could not have existed in the recent past. Moreover, Rosa would know that Kegan's plan was unlikely to succeed. She did not look like the sort of person who could be roused to jealous fury by an event which probably would never happen.

Martineau returned his attention to Kegan. "Just a routine question," he said. "Do you carry insurance on Dessie?"

"I don't, but my wife does," came the prompt reply. "At least, she was still paying the premiums at the time we parted."

"A lot?"

"A couple of bob a week, that's all. I think it comes to about ninety quid when she's sixteen."

"That wouldn't make anybody harm the child, at any rate."

"No," Kegan agreed. "Unless that bloke Jolly can't pay his way. Happen he could be in need of some cash."

"Ninety pounds?"

"Five hundred and ninety," said Kegan steadily.

Martineau looked at him. So it was out. The matter of Dessie's little fortune had been mentioned by one of the two people who could be expected to love her most, and one of the two people who could expect to benefit directly by her death. Martineau thought about that. Would the legacy be divided equally between the parents, or would the father inherit the whole of it? He was not sufficiently well informed about civil law to be sure about it, but he thought that, with or without litigation, the money would be divided. At any rate, the father *appeared* to think so.

"Are you quite certain that half of Dessie's money would go to your wife?" the policeman asked.

"I haven't had legal advice about it, if that's what you mean. I was just assuming it would be a fifty-fifty job."

"Do you really think that Jolly could have done something to Dessie?"

Kegan hesitated, then he said defiantly: "Well, he had as much chance as anybody else, hadn't he? She walks directly past his bit of an office on her way home from school."

"I see," said Martineau. He noticed that Kegan looked strained and haggard. The man showed all the signs of having had a sleepless night. No doubt he was genuinely and deeply worried about Dessie. But did he really think that Jolly could have harmed Dessie, or was it merely his cantankerous nature which was still asserting itself? His dislike of the little bookmaker was strong enough for him to make a slanderous suggestion, even though he knew it to be absurd.

Martineau and Devery departed then, and made their way to Wales Road. At the first fish-and-chip shop they came to, the proprietress informed them that Rosa Vizard, a regular customer, had indeed been in the shop at about fifteen minutes past five on the previous day. Leaving the shop, the two detectives continued to walk along Wales Road. Kegan had said that Dessie would pass Jolly's office on her way from school. They were looking for the office.

One of the side streets was called Leafland Street. They saw that it was a very short street which was made into a dead end by a builder's yard. Near to the entrance of the yard there was a one-story wooden building, quite small but with a fairly big window facing Wales Road. Painted on the lower half of the window was the designation:

SAMUEL JOLLY
TURF ACCOUNTANT
MEMBER OF THE BOOKMAKERS' PROTECTION ASSOCIATION
PHONE BUR 5775

Through the upper half of the window the gray head of an old man could be seen. He was speaking into a telephone. He did not appear to notice the two policemen as they approached.

Martineau tapped on the door of the hut and pushed it open. "Hello there," he said.

The gray head turned, and he saw a small, sharp face. Keen, old eyes looked at him while one pointed ear continued to listen on the phone. The man said: "Right, I'll hear from you later," and put the instrument down. Then he said: "What you want? Police has been here already."

"I suppose they have," said Martineau. "It wouldn't take them long to look around this place, would it?"

"No, it didn't, but I think they saw everythin' there was to see. And they were a long while in the builder's yard."

"M'm. Has Mr. Jolly been here this morning?"

"No. He doesn't come till after his dinner, unless I'm poorly."

"How long does he stay?"

"Till after the racing."

"Was he here between four and five yesterday afternoon?"

"He would be."

"Weren't you here?"

"No. I wasn't so well, and he told me to go home after the three o'clock race."

"He *told* you to go, without your asking?"

"That's right. He's a nice fellow, is Sam."

Martineau thought about that. "It's a nice easy job he's got, four hours a day," he commented.

"It isn't as easy as it looks."

"Perhaps not. And they tell me the bookies have been taking a hiding lately. Favorites winning, and that."

The old man eyed him steadily. "Don't you be kidded, mister. They're not doing so bad. They made enough on the Lincoln and National to retire on, apart from aught else."

"I'm glad to hear it. I'll keep my money in my pocket the next time somebody gives me a horse. Good morning."

The old man nodded and waved in reply as the telephone began to ring. The two policemen left him, and continued their journey in the direction of Mold Street. When they got there, Lucy Kegan saw them approaching her house. She opened the door before they reached it. Martineau thought that she looked ill. He shook his head at her. "Sorry, Mrs. Kegan," he said. "Still no news. I've just come along to make some more inquiries."

"Come in, please," she said.

Sam Jolly was there. Apparently he had just finished an early lunch, the remains of which were still on the table. Martineau guessed that he was ready to go to his office. The day's bets would soon be coming over the telephone with increasing frequency.

But Jolly did not immediately go. He stuck a cigarette into his mouth, lit it, and waited to hear what the police had to say. Martineau came straight to the point.

"I understand you have some life insurance on Dessie, Mrs. Kegan," he said. "I have to find out about that. It's part of police routine."

Mrs. Kegan admitted that she had a policy which included life insurance on Dessie. She produced the policy. Martineau noted the details and thanked her.

"Was it Kegan who told you Lucy had the child insured?" Jolly wanted to know.

"Yes, but only when I specifically asked him about insurance."

"Do you reckon it's some sort of a motive for hurting Dessie?"

"No."

"But her Premium Bond money is a motive, eh?"

"It could be."

Jolly nodded. He rose and went to the sideboard. He opened a drawer and took out a metal cashbox. He unlocked the box and took out a bundle of notes which he thrust casually into the side pocket of his coat. He also took out two small books. "Will you step to the door a minute with me, Inspector?" he asked.

Martineau went outside with him. He opened the books. One

was a Building Society share book which showed that he had three thousand pounds invested, the other was a bank passbook which proved that he was in credit for more than a thousand pounds. "That's just my reserve," he said. "I have nearly six thousand in my business account. I just wanted you to know that nobody in my house is fast for a thousand nicker."

"I understand," said Martineau. "And while we're here you might as well tell me one or two things about yourself. Are you married?"

"Yes."

"Is your wife living in Granchester?"

"I don't know where she's living. She ran off with a fellow ten years ago, when I had nowt. I've never bothered about a divorce, but now Lucy and me are both going to try and get one, with discretion, so's we can get wed. That'll put a stop to Kegan's little plan for getting the custody of Dessie."

"I see. Where were you yesterday afternoon between four and five?"

Jolly's glance met Martineau's. "I was in my office, and I was on my own," he said. "I didn't have a single phone call, either. All the bets I took yesterday were made before four o'clock."

"All right," said the detective. "Thank you."

"Anything else you want to know, just ask me," the bookmaker said. "Now I must be getting off to work." He went and returned his bankbooks to the cashbox, made his adieux, and went away.

Martineau, who had returned to the house with him, asked casually: "Does Mr. Jolly get on all right with Dessie?"

"Never a wrong word," was Mrs. Kegan's instant reply. "You see, it isn't as if she were a lad. He treats her right well. If she wants any extra money for anything she always knows who to ask, and I think he's inclined to spoil her that way. But she knows which side her bread's buttered. She's always willing to run errands for him when he asks her."

"Who bought her the lucky Premium Bond?"

"He did. And he were right pleased when it won."

"He didn't suggest that the money should be his, then?"

"Not he. He's a sportsman. He doesn't look at things that way. He had it put in trust for Dessie."

Martineau nodded rather absently. He looked at his watch. "Thank you," he said. "You'll be informed as soon as there is any news."

He and Devery left her then, and as they walked toward Wales Road he said: "The Flying Dutchman is right handily situated for this job. We'll have a thirst quencher while we compare our impressions of one Samuel Jolly, and then we'll see about getting something to eat."

7.

WHEN he fled after striking Sheila Grayson with his iron bar, Guy Rainer opened a door at the end of the corridor and ran down stone steps into the basement of the school. He went to the outer door of the basement which gave access to that part of the schoolyard which was at the side of the building. He unlocked the door with a piece of strong wire which had already been bent and twisted into shape for the purpose of turning that same lock.

His first panicky intention had been to get right away from the school, but now he perceived that he need not do so. He left the door standing open, to give the impression that he had departed in haste, then he turned back into the basement. He went to the boiler of the school heating plant. It had hidden him before, when the police had searched the place, and he could see no reason why it should not hide him again.

It was a big, old, Cornish boiler, firmly mounted on a brick base. In winter it was heated by coke or coal; in summer it was, of course, quite cold. It was cold now, and it had already been given its annual cleaning. The firebox door stood open, the bars were clean, and the flue beyond was not too dirty. He crawled along the firebox, the length of the boiler, until he came to the beginning of the flue. There, beneath the level of the firebox, was a sort of well or ash pit, which apparently had been emptied when the flue was cleaned. There was just enough room for Guy to sit there, hugging his knees in almost total darkness, hidden from the view of anyone who might flash the light of a torch along the firebox.

He waited there, moderately confident of remaining undiscovered. The police had not found him during their first, routine search. Now, because he had given them a reason for believing that he was not in the building at all, he hoped that their second search would not be more thorough.

The expected search party arrived. Guy heard voices. Eventually a beam of light hit the sooty iron wall above his head as someone looked into the firebox. He heard a man say: "Could a fellow crawl through there?" and he began to sweat. He did not hear the answer. Feet thumped on the top of the boiler, and then there was silence.

Guy crouched in the boiler for nearly two hours, and then he emerged because he could bear the confinement no longer. He climbed out very quietly and carefully, then stood in the gloom listening. The basement was as silent as a tomb. He sat down on the concrete floor and removed his heavy prison boots. He tied the boots firmly by their laces to the back of his belt. Then, silent as a cat in his thick woolen socks, he began to reconnoiter.

Now, he guessed, the police would know where he had got the boiler suit he was wearing. He had found it here in the basement, hanging on a nail. They would also know that here he had found his iron bar. They would perhaps also know that he had been finding food in the school kitchen. They would be very suspicious about himself and the school, even though he had left a door open to make them believe that he had gone away. He thought they might have left one or two men in the school, to lie in wait for him.

He noiselessly examined the outer door of the basement. Now it was locked, and it was also bolted on the inside. If the police thought that he had fled from the school, they were making sure that he did not return to it by that door. If they suspected that he might still be in the school, they were making sure that he could not depart by that door without leaving evidence of his departure. Also, possibly, there would be a policeman outside, concealed in some position which would give him a view of the door.

He toured the basement and assured himself that it was deserted, then he cautiously approached the dusty stone steps which climbed to corridor level. The cellar-head door was closed. He did not touch it, but he could see in the crack of daylight between door and jamb that it was not locked. He listened, and heard nothing.

He crouched to peer between the worn doorstep and the bottom of the door. He could see a few of the maple blocks of the corridor floor and the foot of the partition on the other side of the corridor, and that was all.

It was another sense which warned him of danger. There was an odor which seemed infinitely delicious as his nostrils conveyed it to his craving palate. On the other side of the door, quite near, some person was smoking a cigarette. The human element again, he thought. During the quiet hours of waiting, the policeman in the corridor was treating himself to a forbidden cigarette. Guy coolly reflected that the top copper should have expected such a thing to happen. He should have known that there was no scent more alien to the corridor of a junior school than the smell of tobacco. That smell would linger for hours. The top copper should have posted a nonsmoker in the corridor.

Silently Guy withdrew into the basement. He thought about the top copper, and visualized Martineau. He imagined that he could read Martineau's mind through his actions. The chief inspector assumed that if his quarry was still in the school, then he was somewhere in the basement. So he had posted men to make sure that he would be arrested when he came up for air.

Also, Guy thought with sudden fear, there might be yet another search of the basement: a surprise search. The police might not have been fooled by the open door. They might come thundering down the steps at any moment. Fumbling with haste, he put on his boots. He crawled into the boiler again. "Get back into the cheese," he mocked himself for his fear. "Crawl under your stone, you worm."

He had counted an hour away when he was startled by a flash of light above his head. He had heard nothing. He reflected that it was indeed a surprise search, conducted without noise. This time the feet did not thump along the top of the boiler, they padded along. He heard nothing more than that. He waited a further half-hour, then he climbed out of the boiler and stretched painfully. Now at least, he thought, the police would think that he was not in the building. Would they still maintain their watch? If they did, how the devil was he going to get out of there?

He thought about that. He did not want to leave the basement before darkness came. He had plenty of time to find a way out, if there was one. But he thought that he had better start looking for it immediately, while the sunshine of outdoors was penetrating every grating and crack to give him light.

Once more he toured the basement. He studied the coal chute, and realized that if he went out that way he would make some noise. He examined a row of small windows whose tops were only a few inches above ground level. Their tiny areas were protected by iron gratings. The windows opened outward, so that they could not be opened without first going outside and removing the gratings. Deep in thought, he returned to the boiler.

He wondered if the boiler itself would provide a way out of the basement. A boiler like this would have a fairly wide chimney, he surmised. It should be rather like a small mill chimney.

Then where was the chimney? He could not remember. He could not remember seeing a chimney on the school.

Twenty years is a long time, he reflected. He had forgotten where the chimney was. In his mind's eye he saw the exterior of the school, and one thing he became sure of, there was no chimney pot visible from the street or from the school yard. Still, there had to be a chimney.

He concentrated. In one place, he remembered, the school was three stories high. It was an architectural oddity, just a single higher room which in his day had been a storeroom. It had windows on three sides. And on the fourth? There was the chimney! He remembered the peculiar appearance of the roof from a distance. There was an open chimney, oblong in shape, and of considerable dimensions.

He went up the steps at the side of the boiler. He walked on top of it. There was a narrow, low tunnel beyond the boiler. This was where the searching policemen had gone, to look in the tunnel. He went along in darkness, feeling his way. The tunnel widened. He risked striking a match from a box which he had found in the school kitchen, and he saw that he was in a small, dusty brick chamber about five feet high. Facing him was a vertical manhole cover, held in place by a thick iron bar. He removed the bar, and the iron cover fell toward him.

He lifted the cover aside, and looked into the chimney. He estimated that it was two and a half feet by four feet. The end of the flue was four feet below him. He craned to look upward, and saw an oblong patch of light fifty feet above his head. This, then, was his way out, if he could make the climb.

He backed out of the manhole and replaced the cover. He struck another match to see if he had left everything in order, and remembered, with a feeling that he had been fortunate in doing so, to pick up the spent match which he had already discarded. He returned to the front of the boiler and sat down to wait, ready to crawl into the firebox at the first sign of another search.

He now thought that he would be able to get out of the school, which had become just another prison to him. He wanted to go away from there, as he would want to leave any place which was guarded. But where would he go? Where could he hide until the police came to the conclusion that he had escaped from the district?

He assumed that on every crossroads for a mile around there would be policemen in plain clothes. He was also aware that, apart from a very few close friends, no one in the neighborhood who knew him would be prepared to help him. Probably the first person who recognized him would raise a hue-and-cry, because the collective mind of the general public believed that he was responsible for the disappearance of Dessie Kegan. Had that child been found? He hoped so, he fervently hoped so. He was discouraged by the thought that every man's hand would be against him until the mystery of Dessie was solved. The thought made him feel tired, and he began to see how a fugitive could become so weary and uncertain that he would voluntarily surrender.

Until he got some decent clothes, every move he made would have to be made in the dark. Every move where? The docks were a mile away, and if he wanted to get on board a suitable ship he would have to reconnoiter in daylight. With regard to the matter of sailing overseas, he would want to know where he was going.

Though he was not by nature a thief, he was prepared to steal in order to remain free. That he accepted as a condition of outlawry. He would steal whatever he needed whenever he could.

A man on the run usually has no alternative but to steal, but Guy in his home town did have an alternative. He could try to get friends to help him. There were two at least whom he believed he could trust. He could make contact with one of them by telephone, if he could get to a phone. There was a pay telephone in the school corridor, but he had been unable to find the necessary pennies. There would be another phone in the headmaster's

71

study, but the study door had a lock which was too good to be opened by a piece of wire.

Until he could seek the aid of friends, Guy thought about likely hiding places in the neighborhood. The nearest was Holly Lodge, where once he had nearly been caught. The scramble through that overgrown garden had ended his first attempt to get to the docks. Beyond Holly Lodge, on the other side of Wales Road, was Markham's Mill. He did not know much about the interior of the mill, but he had been chased out of the mill yard a few times as a lad. The boilerhouse, he remembered, was a single-story brick lean-to. He could get on the roof there. It might lead him somewhere. He might find a window which he could open with the penknife which he had taken from Sheila Grayson's desk. He might find a door with an old-fashioned lock which could be turned by his piece of wire. He decided that he would try to get to Markham's Mill. It would be a dangerous journey, but then his entire existence as a free man was precarious.

He was not desperately hungry, but he was very thirsty. There was a faucet near the foot of the basement steps, but it was a noisy one. He dared not risk using it while there was a policeman in the corridor above. Squatting beside the boiler, he licked his dry lips and compared his present circumstances and prospects with those of a few years ago. In those days he had been young and free, with a job which he liked and a girl he adored. It seemed to him, thinking of those times, that he should have been continuously happy every hour of every day. And being honest with himself, he admitted that he had only been as happy as his disposition would allow. He had had a good job, but he had grumbled with his mates about matters which now seemed to be infinitely petty. He had resented criticism, and he had fumed for hours over a sharp word from a foreman or a boss, and sometimes his flaring temper had got the better of him on such occasions. Also, though he had loved Patricia Grayson, he had quarreled with her a number of times. They had quarreled about nothing, he remembered now. After such quarrels, his black moods had been suicidal. Suicide over a wench? He grinned in the darkness. He must have been daft, he decided. He hadn't known when he was well off. Come to think of it, he hadn't been a lot happier than he was now, in a position which was well-nigh hopeless and with many dangers and difficulties ahead. He was thirsty, tired, dirty, penniless and dying for a smoke, but at least he was free. On the day that he had killed a man he had lost most of the things which men fear to lose. So he had lost his fear of losing them, and he thought then that he would never want them back. Only freedom he wanted, and that he had regained.

There was one aspect of the matter upon which he would not allow himself to dwell. He would not admit that his was only the freedom of a hunted fox. Henceforth he would always be in danger, whereas if he had stayed to serve his sentence he would eventually have earned the real freedom to look a man in the eye and announce his identity; the freedom of having nothing to hide. Henceforth, if he remained at liberty, he would no longer be Guy Rainer. He would be a shy, retiring character by the name of Tom Robinson or Herbert Smith: always quiet, always unostentatious, always anxious to avoid trouble. In former days, along with the great majority of mankind, he had occasionally known the fear of losing a good job or a good name. That fear did not trouble him now, but if he succeeded in assuming a new identity it would be replaced by one infinitely worse, the constant dread of being involved in trouble and being pushed into the limelight. Just then, that did not occur to him. Had it done so, he would have declined to think about it.

Of course he regretted the incident which had, in the conventional sense, ruined his life. He had been a fool to kill Bert Shell. He ought to have given him a damned good hiding and left it at that. But the man's callous defiance and his own red temper and the poker within reach had made manslaughter terribly easy. He remembered that he had always been jealous of Pat Grayson. She had been a girl of frivolous ways, likely to provoke a possessive lover. She had had a roving eye. Perhaps he had always known subconsciously that she would eventually be unfaithful to him. He remembered that he had often burned with anger when it had been merely a possibility in his mind. In a sense, Pat and her roving eye had conditioned him for murder.

He knew now that he had chosen the wrong girl. He knew that Sheila had always liked him. She would have been his for the asking. But he had looked at her with eyes which were dazzled by her splendid sister. He had counted himself lucky when Pat had accepted him as her fiancé; now he knew that he had been unlucky. He would have been happier with the younger sister.

He guessed that Sheila would not like him very much now, since he had struck her with a crowbar. He was thankful that it had been a glancing blow. He might have killed her. That would have been terrible. Also, he might have killed Martineau last night, if he had not had the presence of mind to aim lower than the crown of his head. That little crowbar was a dangerous thing, too hard and too heavy for hitting people on the head. He knew that he ought to get rid of it. He also knew that he would not do so until he had found a better weapon. The thing fitted into the rule pocket of his "borrowed" boiler suit, but it was really too heavy to be carried that way. It hampered him when he was running or climbing.

He realized now that Sheila had not intended to betray him. She had merely been determined that he should not hurt her sister. She had perceived that discovery was inevitable as soon as Pat appeared. Pat's instinctive flight had shown that she at least had no sympathy with him. He supposed that he owed Sheila an apology, a most humble apology.

Time passed. The dim light in the basement faded. Guy wondered if there would be another search of the cellar before dark. It was unlikely, but the thought of it made him uneasy. He crawled into the boiler. He counted an hour and a half in there—5,400 seconds—and heard nothing. He came out and stretched himself. Soon, he thought, it would be time to go.

He considered his route. Holly Road was out of the question. Apart from the policemen who would almost certainly be watching, there would be a number of ordinary people. In the state he would be in when he had climbed out of the chimney, he would not be able to let *anybody* see him. On this side of Holly Road, between the school and Holly Lodge, there were the houses of which Dr. Kennedy's was one. Behind the gardens of the houses there was a ditch, which would be dry in this sort of weather. The ditch could be a way to Holly Lodge, if it was not guarded. On the other side of the ditch was St. Mary's Church, and it might be possible to get to Holly Lodge by crawling between the ancient gravestones in the churchyard. In any case it would be a difficult journey. There would have to be not one unnecessary sound or one unconsidered action.

He grew tired of waiting. He mounted the steps beside the boiler, made his way to the manhole, removed the cover and climbed into the chimney.

8.

WHEN Martineau and Devery walked into the Flying Dutchman Inn shortly after noon, they found that the bar was as busy as any bar might be on a Saturday. The bouncing barmaid served them with a smile, but she had no time to talk. Many of the customers stared at them when they entered, knowing them for what they were. Then the hubbub of conversation, which had temporarily died, gradually regained its normal volume.

The two detectives drank their beer and looked around. John Kegan was standing alone at the further end of the bar, morosely staring at the glass of whisky and chaser of beer in front of him.

All the other customers were strangers to them. Moreover they were all quite at ease, men and women who had no reason to fear the police. Martineau quickly finished his drink and put down his glass. "The beer's good, at any rate," he said. "I'll phone for a car and we'll wait for it outside."

The car took them to Headquarters, where Martineau reported to Clay and briefly informed him of the morning's work.

"Jolly automatically goes on your list, then," the superintendent commented.

"I'm afraid so, sir. What does Sergeant Bird say about Miss Grayson's letter?"

"He's found three different specimens of prints, none of them on our files. On the letter itself, a good thumb and forefinger which probably were made by the writer, also some faint dabs which might belong to Miss Grayson. On the envelope there are three overlaid, no good at all. We assume they belong to the writer, Miss Grayson, and the postman."

"We've got something to go on, then, if we find the writer and get his dabs."

"That is so," Clay agreed.

Martineau left him then, and rejoined Devery. Together they looked at the daybook. They perceived that the Granchester City Police had been mobilized for an emergency. All leave had been canceled, and the men of the uniform branch were on duty for twelve hours a day. The men of the C.I.D., of course, would be working anything up to eighteen hours a day, and some of the most senior ranks of the force even longer than that.

Various and numerous reports from civilian sources were briefly noted in the book. Men who might have been Guy Rainer and little girls who might have been Dessie Kegan had been seen here and there all over the city and its great spread of suburbs and satellite towns. The marginal initials in the book showed that all these reports had been or were being investigated. There was plenty to do.

Martineau sighed. "Ten thousand false alarms," he said. "Let's go and see what's on the menu today."

Feeling refreshed and rested after a meal and a cup of coffee, the two men ordered a car and rode to the divisional police station whose personnel had the honor of including the less well-behaved inhabitants of Burnside in their responsibilities. They dismissed the car and entered the station. There they were met by the superintendent of the division, who was tired and baggy-eyed after working all through the day and the night.

"Hello, Martineau," he said with a yawn. "Do you know anything of note?"

The detective shrugged and shook his head.

"You're handling the family end of the business," the superintendent persisted. "Haven't you got a suspect?"

"For what?"

"For murder. We're going to find this child dead, you know. Dead and buried, maybe."

"I'm afraid you're right, sir," Martineau admitted.

"And you're seeking information and getting ready to crack the job when it is a job. And keeping it all in the C.I.D."

"If I knew anything which would help you or anybody else, I'd spill it. Nobody is hogging this job. No sir!"

The superintendent grinned. "I wouldn't trust the C.I.D. as far as I could throw a double-decker bus," he said. "What do you want?"

"Could I see your key book?"

"Sure," said the superintendent amiably. "And if you can find any places where we haven't looked already, good luck to you." He called for the book, which contained the names and addresses of people who carried the keys of lock-up premises in the division. It had been compiled so that the police could always reach a responsible person at night in the event of insecure premises, a break-in, a fire or other damage.

From the book Martineau read out names and addresses pertaining to most of the lock-up places in the Wales Road–Holly Road–Eden Street area, while Devery wrote them down.

"I feel better equipped now," said the chief inspector when the work was done. "We'll just take a stroll as far as Collier Street and see what's going on."

They walked the short distance from the police station to Wales Road, a section of the road which was not a part of Dessie Kegan's route from school. They turned toward that part, not hurrying but moving steadily along and looking at people and places. They approached the Flying Dutchman Inn, and out of the inn, apparently trying to emulate the action suggested by the inn sign, sailed John Kegan. He surged out of the doorway, turned suddenly and was taken aback, looked blindly around, and then set an unsteady course toward home. He was, evidently, very drunk or very ill.

"Well, well," said Martineau. "He's full. It's running out of his ears."

"It'll be running out of his eyes in a minute," said Devery. "Did you see his face, all twisted up? One kind word and he'll be a crying drunk."

"That probably means he's going to kick hell out of somebody quite soon. I'll walk gently along behind him. You go in there and talk to the barmaid."

Devery entered the inn. The time was twenty-five minutes past two. There was a burr of conversation and a rattle of dominoes in the taproom, but the bar customers had all gone home. The barmaid was polishing a glass, and a cigarette burned on a tray beside her.

"Hello," she said. "Lost your pal?"

"He's busy elsewhere," said Devery lightly, "so I seized the chance to come and talk to the bonniest barmaid in Burnside."

"Nice of you, but I don't kid as easy as that. Jack Kegan goes out, you come in. Have you been following him around?"

"No, and that's the truth. As far as I know, Kegan isn't suspected of any crime."

"I should think not. He wouldn't hurt his own kid. What shall I get you?"

"Just a half of bitter. Will you have something?"

"It'll cost you if I do. I'd like a gin."

"A pleasure. Poor old Kegan. I expect he's taken to the drink because he can't stand the strain."

"I reckon that's it. And a bit of trouble at home."

"With the beautiful Rosa? You don't say!"

"Do you think she's beautiful?" asked the barmaid, swiftly sidetracked by the mention of another woman's looks.

Devery soon had her back on the main line. "That was just a manner of speaking," he said shamelessly. "She's not half as lovely as you are. What has she been doing?"

"She's said something to upset Jack, I don't know what."

"Didn't he tell you?"

The girl hesitated. Then she said: "It's nothing, really. Rosa is keen on having a good time. She likes new clothes, and going to the seaside and that. She hasn't had any good times lately. Last year they never went anywhere because the baby was so little. She didn't get any new clothes, either. Jack wouldn't give her the money. Said he couldn't afford."

"So she set up a moan this morning, just at the wrong time. Was that it?"

"Something of the sort. And she's got somebody who's promised to look after the baby while they go away for a week. She must have been that pleased she came right out with it, and said something about writing off to Blackpool for lodgings. He thought it was sinful to talk about holidays while little Dessie was still missing. He stamped out of the house and went on a rant. He's had a fair lot here. The boss came in and stopped his tap for him just now, so he cleared off."

"Rather tactless of Rosa," Devery commented. "She could have waited until something was known about Dessie."

"Rosa doesn't believe in waiting for what she wants. Not a minute longer than she has to, at any rate."

"H'm. Is Kegan normally a heavy drinker?"

"I wouldn't say he was. He only seems to drink at week-ends."

"And then does he go it a bit?"

"Not really. He's same as other fellows on a Saturday night: excitable and talkative after a few pints. Ready for bother, sometimes. Easily led away, happen. But I don't think there's much harm in him."

Devery thought of Kegan's hot, fanatical eyes. Easily led away? By a woman, perhaps. Through vanity and the gratification of instinct. But he would have certain fixed ideas which nobody would be able to change. A woman at her most seductive might change him temporarily perhaps, but eventually she would be back where she started.

"Can you remember something?" the detective asked. "When Kegan left his wife, did he take Dessie with him?"

"I believe he did," the girl answered. "The mother was in a rare state. She went to court for a separation and got the custody."

Devery nodded. It was as he had thought. One of the permanent things in Kegan's mind was his attitude to Dessie. He loved the child. But this was not the normal love of a father for a daughter, the love which makes a man tread his shoes straight in order to make sure that the girl has a decent upbringing and the sense of security which comes from living in a well-ordered home. Kegan could not have been thinking of anything like that when he took the child into the home of Rosa Vizard. Apparently he just wanted her, without any real consideration for her ultimate welfare. A less bigoted man would have realized long ago that the child was better with her mother.

Yes, Devery decided as he treated himself to a second glass of beer, Kegan was well-meaning perhaps, but he was capable of strange behavior in matters concerning his daughter.

While the sergeant drank his beer and tried to get more information from the barmaid, Martineau sauntered along Wales Road and observed the halting progress of Kegan. Passers-by

looked at the drunken man with various expressions of pity, contempt and disgust. They also got out of his way. He tottered
heedlessly across the road, and arrived at the other side by the
courtesy of a number of careful drivers. He stopped at the end
of Leafland Street, because he wanted to, and not because his
legs refused to take him further. He stared at Sam Jolly's wooden
hut, and then he stared at the ground in front of him. Had he
been capable of meditating, that was what he would have been
doing. Perhaps his stupefied brain slept for a moment, because
quite suddenly he lurched horribly and nearly fell. When he had
recovered his balance, he had forgotten whatever it was he had
been trying to elucidate. He gazed about in a puzzled manner,
and then went reeling on his way.

Martineau followed, and passing Leafland Street he also
looked at the hut. Jolly was not at the window. Had he been
there, Kegan would probably have gone to him. With what intention? Martineau wondered. To say or do something of meaning
and importance, or merely to assail the man with drunken abuse?

Kegan reached the crossroads. He stopped there, and peered
across Eden Street at Markham's Mill as if he had never seen it
before. He reached and caught the arm of a young woman who
passed, and tried to say something to her. She snatched her arm
away, and ran from him. He shook his head sadly at such treatment of himself, then staggered into Eden Street.

Martineau lingered on the corner, letting Kegan get further
ahead. The sight of a drunken man would not be a sensation in
Collier Street, but temporarily Kegan was a figure in the news.
The eyes of the street would be upon him, and furthermore there
might be a reporter. Now that he had left the main road, Martineau did not want to be seen following him. It would be better
to appear on the street a minute or two after he had gone
indoors.

When Martineau did turn the corner to walk along Collier
Street he saw that it was as he had expected it to be. The neighbors, mainly women, were at their doors and windows, watching

and listening with lively interest. When he came in sight they turned their heads to watch him, knowing him quite well by name and reputation.

Also, as he had expected, there was trouble at No. 11. There was a dull crash, as if somebody had picked up an article of furniture and thrown it. This was followed by a louder crash which was a mixture of sounds, a consonance of the noises of damage. That, Martineau decided as he approached, was the master of the house kicking the table over.

Then the voice of Rosa was heard, above the crying of the child. "You bloody rotter! Look at my new teapot!"

Kegan's reply was not loud, but now Martineau was much nearer to the open door. "Decent—decent woman would sided table long since," the drunken man said thickly. "Tha'll teash you not leave stuff on table all day."

"Get to hell out of here, you sodden ruin! Get you to bed and sleep it off!"

"My Dessie. Lost my little Dessie, and you don't care," Kegan said.

Martineau was at the door then. He had already decided that he was not going to overhear anything of importance. He showed himself in the doorway, but nobody was looking at him. He saw Kegan go rubber-legged around the overturned table and collapse with closed eyes and a groan of relief on the settee, and sink immediately into deep slumber. He heard a slight metallic sound, and he stepped into the house. Rosa, gibbering with rage, had picked up the poker and was advancing toward the settee. Martineau caught her upraised arm and gently took the poker from her. "Steady," he said. "That won't do any good."

The distraught woman leaned on him and wept. "The beast," she sobbed. "The drunken beast." He guided her to an armchair, and sat her down. Then he put the table on its legs, and began to replace articles which were not broken. The baby stopped crying and stared at him. He made a chuckling noise at the baby and it smiled. He went and found a long-handled brush and swept up the broken pots, and all the time he did this he made noises and pulled faces until the child was crowing with pleasure. When he had done he found that even Rosa was smiling faintly.

"You're good with babies," she said.

"I'm good with some babies," he admitted. "Others are scared to death of me."

"Thank you for sweeping up," she said.

"Oh, I just did it to pass the time, until you had calmed down a bit."

"I don't know what I'd have done if you hadn't stopped me."

"Oh, I don't suppose you would have hurt him. You might have laid the poker across his backside once or twice."

"I was absolutely wild. Even if Dessie *is* missing, why does he have to take it out of me and *my* baby?"

"That's the way it goes with some fellows. Perhaps you said something which upset him, earlier on."

"I did not. I've been proper tactful ever since—ever since yesterday. He was all right when he went out."

Martineau became certain then. His earlier impression was confirmed. He was not going to get any information out of this incident. He glanced at Kegan, who was snoring. "He'll probably be all right again when he wakes up," he said as a preliminary to departure. The woman could be safely left now. The mood of violence was ended.

As he moved toward the door she said: "Well, I'm certainly glad you called." Her voice and smile were friendly. Very friendly. Inviting, he thought.

"I'll call again sometime," he said.

Her smile widened. She made eyes at him, and he reflected that she was not the sort of girl who would let her association with Kegan stop her from having an affair with another man.

He said "Cheerio," and as he walked away from the house he asked himself: "Bedroom eyes, Martineau? Or are you kidding yourself? Or is she kidding you?"

9.

WHEN Sergeant Devery left the Flying
Dutchman Inn at ten minutes to three that afternoon he walked
along Wales Road with the intention of finding Chief Inspector
Martineau and rejoining him. He expected to find him somewhere in the vicinity of Collier Street.

Walking on the left side of the road, he passed the entrance to
the public gardens known as Burnside Park. As he passed he
casually noted a fine display of spring flowers in a circular bed
near the gate. Coming along the path which rounded the other
side of the bed of flowers was Albert Vizard, and he did not
appear to have seen Devery. The sergeant considered that to be
fortunate, and he took a skip and a jump to get past the gateway
and out of sight.

Albert had been walking briskly, looking about him and behind. Devery thought that he had detected furtiveness and sub-
dued glee in his gait and demeanor, as if he were restraining an
urge to run giggling on tiptoe. Devery had seen that sort of thing
before, in the bearing of boys after some piece of mischief, and in
the bearing of thieves in the joyful interval between the acquisi-
tion of someone else's property and the policeman's tap on the
shoulder. "Albert has just done something," he surmised. "Albert
has just done something in the park."

Beside the wall of the park there was no cover for the detective, but on the other side of the road were shops and people. He
sprinted across, and he was trying to make himself small in a
group of people at a bus stop when Albert emerged from the
park. Albert paused at the curb, looked all around him and behind him, then began to cross the road toward the bus stop.
While he was avoiding an approaching car, and watching the car,

84

Devery turned away and dived into the nearest shop, which advertised itself as Burnside Medical Stores.

There were no customers in the shop. Devery moved well back into the interior, away from the counter, and watched Albert join the bus queue. The man behind the counter looked at him in a surprised and slightly apprehensive way. "Some sort of trouble, sir?" he asked.

"Maybe, but not for you," said the sergeant, showing his warrant card and not shifting his gaze from Albert. "I just want to stand here a minute."

"Police," the man said with some relief as he peered at the card. "That's all right, stand there as long as you like. We'll all feel happier when that fellow Rainer is caught."

They stood in silence, the man looking curiously from Devery to the bus queue. Devery watched Albert. Albert looked along the road for a bus. His mouth was puckered, as if he were whistling under his breath. Inner satisfaction could be discerned behind a face which was trying to be as stolid as a face in a bus queue ought to be. "He's the cat who's had the cream," Devery decided. "He's feeling pretty good. He's done something, all right."

Then Albert left the queue. He stepped from the curb and flagged a vehicle. A taxi came to a stop beside him. Devery moved to the shop door and looked through the glass pane. He made a mental note of the cab's Hackney Carriage number as Albert stepped into it.

The taxi moved off. Assuming that its passenger would be looking out of the rear window, Devery stayed in the shop until it was at a safe distance from him. Then he said, "Thanks. Cheerio," to the man behind the counter and stepped out to the street. He moved to the curb. A bus was in sight. Albert had taken a cab when he had less than half a minute to wait for a bus. For a man with only two days' wages in his pocket, that seemed to be a rather extravagant thing to do.

A Ford Zephyr the color of ivory overtook the approaching

bus. The driver of the Ford had no passengers. Devery stepped into the road and waved energetically to him, and at the same time he pointed to the bus. The Ford stopped, and the driver, looking rather alarmed, turned to stare back along the road.

Devery stepped to the car and opened the near side front door. He had his warrant card in his hand. "Excuse the tricky tactics, sir," he said. "I had to stop you. I am a police officer on duty and I need your help. Can I ride a little way with you?"

"Get in," the man said. "You scared me. I thought I'd hit something without knowing it."

"I'm sorry. I didn't want you to ignore my signal."

"That's all right," the man said. He was a slim, alert-looking man about forty years of age, wearing a blue blazer and flannels. "Is it anything to do with that little girl who is missing around here?"

"That's the inquiry I'm on at the moment."

"I think I know how somebody must be feeling about that child. I have two daughters of my own. I'm at your disposal the whole of the afternoon if you want me, and only too glad to help."

"You're at liberty all afternoon?"

"Yes. I *was* going to watch a bit of cricket, but that's neither here nor there."

Devery could not yet see Albert's taxi. "Go a little faster if you can," he said. "I'll see that you don't get booked for speeding."

The driver showed that he could go a good deal faster. Presently Devery saw the taxi, still going straight along Wales Road, heading for the heart of Granchester. Soon he was near enough to read the Hackney Carriage number.

"See that cab?" he said. "Let him pull away from you a bit. That's right. Now just keep him in sight."

"This is the sort of stuff you see at the pictures," the driver said, with a certain glee.

Devery grinned. "Don't be disappointed if the man in the cab *is* only going to the pictures," he said.

"Yes. I suppose you get lots of promising leads which tail off to nothing. What's your particular interest in this man, or shouldn't I ask?"

"There's no harm in you asking, but I'm afraid I can't tell you anything at the moment. But if it's any consolation to you, I think I'm on to something good. Neither of us is wasting his time."

"It's enough to know that I'm being of some practical help," said the driver, satisfied.

The taxi went on into the city. The car trailed it at a discreet distance. The driver introduced himself as Robert Campbell, a man in the leather trade.

The taxi stopped at the public library. The following car was stopped by traffic lights, but it was near enough for its occupants to have the taxi under observation. As Albert alighted and paid the fare, Devery said: "Take a good look at him. He's the one we're after."

The taxi drove on to the rank beside the Royal Lancaster Hotel. Albert stood on the curb, looking around, then he turned and entered the library.

The traffic lights changed color. Campbell drove over the crossing and stopped. "What now?" he asked.

Devery looked at him in new appraisal, and said: "Now's your chance to do a bit of detective work, if you feel like it."

"I'll have a bash. Do you want me to follow him in there and see what he's doing?"

"Yes. He knows me, you see. I'll tag along well in rear, in case something develops."

"Let's go, then," said Campbell, starting to get out of the car. He went across to the library and entered. Devery followed about twenty yards behind.

Inside the library, Campbell strolled along the wide central hall, apparently looking at the doors on either side, in search of a particular department. In reality, of course, he was looking for

Albert. Devery, watching him from just inside the door, thought that he played his part very well.

The library was moderately busy, as might have been expected on a Saturday afternoon. There may have been fifty people in the hall, but Albert was not one of them. Campbell turned, and made a slight gesture of helplessness. Devery answered by pointing at the door of the reference library. Campbell nodded, and sauntered toward the door.

Devery's guess had been a good one. Albert was in the reference library, staring at a section of lawbooks. Campbell walked to a nearby section, chose a book at random, and went to sit at a table. He opened the book and read not a word of it.

If Albert was seeking information upon a point of law, he obviously had not much idea how to find it. He frowned at the books, picking volumes from the shelves and glancing at them briefly and ineffectively before he returned them. He wandered from end to end of the section. Finally he grew tired of squinting at titles. He selected an armful of books and took them to a table. After spending about ten minutes over them, he returned them to their places. Once more he scrutinized titles, then turned abruptly away and caught Campbell looking at him.

Campbell did not lose his composure. He knew that he was not at all like a policeman in appearance. He merely changed the focus of his eyes, so that he stared pensively through Vizard and beyond him.

"By gum," said Vizard. "No wonder they say the law is made by lawyers for lawyers. I reckon to be middling intelligent, but I'm blowed if I can find what I'm looking for. Are *you* any good at delving in lawbooks?"

Campbell's gaze settled stern and cold upon Vizard. He did not speak, but pointed to a prominent notice which stated in plain terms that speech was forbidden in the reference room.

Vizard sneered, and walked out. When he was gone, Campbell cautiously went to the door and peered into the hall. He saw Vizard making for the entrance, but he could see nothing of

Devery. He let Vizard move out of sight before he emerged from the reference room. Then he saw Devery step out of another doorway.

Devery beckoned, and walked rapidly to the entrance. His companion joined him there. They looked out, and saw Vizard stepping briskly away in the direction of Somerset Square.

"We'll give him a few seconds start," said Devery, "then we'll follow in the car."

In the car, watching Vizard as he bustled along, the policeman asked: "What was he after?"

"He was looking at lawbooks, but I don't think he found what he wanted. He didn't seem to have any idea how to look for it."

"Could he have hidden something in a book?"

"I suppose so, but I didn't see anything to make me think so."

"It isn't likely, anyway. It was just a thought. Did you see the titles of any of the books he opened?"

"No, I wasn't near enough. He spoke to me, though."

"He did?" Devery was surprised. "What did he say?"

Campbell told him. The policeman said: "You did very well," but something in his voice made the other man turn to look at him.

They rode on in silence. Campbell frowned in thought. Suddenly he took one hand from the wheel and slapped his forehead. "I'm an ass," he said. "I should have asked him what he wanted to know, and pretended to help him."

"Don't worry about that. I doubt if he would have told you anything important."

Campbell was relieved. "He wouldn't?"

"No."

"Then I didn't do so bad after all."

"You did all right," said Devery.

They were in Somerset Square. They saw Vizard cross the square and go to the taxi rank, but the last taxi moved away before he reached it. He turned round and walked a hundred yards to the bus terminus in the square. He stepped onto a waiting bus.

The driver and the conductor of the bus were standing near the driver's cabin. Devery saw the conductor light a cigarette. From that he assumed that the bus would not be pulling out immediately.

"Drive round and stop beside that row of phone boxes," he said. Then he said: "Sorry. I'm ordering you about as if you were a copper."

"That's all right," said Campbell. He stopped beside the row of kiosks, in such a position that he and his car were hidden from anyone looking out of the window of the stationary bus.

Devery found an unoccupied kiosk and stepped inside. He dialed the Headquarters number, and decided that he had better speak to Chief Superintendent Clay. He told his story to Clay, who understood what he meant when he said that Vizard, emerging from the park, had had the look of a man who had "just done something." He went on: "He's sitting in a bus now. He may be heading for home. I'm in doubt whether to collar him now and turn him up for what he's got, or wait and see where he goes."

Clay's voice came to him, gruffly excited. "Burnside Park, you said? There's another thing just come in, and it might tie up with Vizard. You'd better wait and see where he goes, and whatever you do, don't let him give you the slip."

As Martineau was walking away from Collier Street after his interview with Rosa Vizard, he noticed in Eden Street that the main gate to the yard of Markham's Mill stood wide-open. He looked into the yard. A handsome car stood there, and two men who were certainly not of the laboring type were discussing a big heap of old, broken-up loom frames. It appeared that a metal merchant was about to offer a price for scrap.

He went into the yard and gazed around. He wondered if anything had happened to a child in there. Or could a hunted man be hiding there? He went to the two men and spoke to them, introducing himself. One of them was the manager of the mill.

"Yes, the place was thoroughly searched just before dark yesterday," the manager said in answer to his question. "It's been locked up ever since. All was secure when I looked around this morning. Have a look yourself if you like."

"Thanks, I'll just nose around a bit if you don't mind," said Martineau.

He walked round the outside of the mill, examining doors and windows, and noticing locks which might not be inviolable to the man who had been able to open the basement door of Burnside School. He also noticed that an agile man might be able to get on to the roof of the weaving shed by way of the boilerhouse roof. Otherwise he saw nothing to arouse his suspicions: Burnside was full of mills and workshops which were just as vulnerable. He walked out of the yard and went along to the crossroads. He looked along Wales Road. Devery was not yet in sight.

He sauntered along Wales Road, expecting to meet the sergeant, but instead he met another of his men, Detective Constable Cassidy.

"I've just had an inquiry in Barmouth Street," Cassidy explained. "A woman said she saw Guy Rainer looking through her bedroom window this morning at cockcrow. I don't know why a man would climb a drain pipe just to look at her. She's sixty if she's a day. But there it is. Who am I to say she didn't see him?"

"It'll give her something to talk about," said Martineau tolerantly. "You'd better come with me now."

They walked along together, and as they passed the end of Leafland Street Martineau glanced in the direction of Sam Jolly's office. The bookmaker was standing near the window, looking out. He saw Martineau, and waved in a beckoning way.

"You stay here and look out for Sergeant Devery," the chief inspector said to Cassidy. "I'll go and see what this chap wants."

He went to the hut, and Jolly met him outside the door. "Afternoon, Inspector," he said, looking hopeful. "Any news?"

"No good news, at any rate," was the reply.

Jolly looked at his watch. He had an air of anxiety or disappointment. He looked down at the ground in an undecided way. Martineau waited.

"I thought Dessie might be back home, safe and sound," said Jolly at last.

"Why did you think that?"

Jolly looked over his shoulder, and looking past him Martineau discerned his little clerk sitting on a stool in a corner of the hut.

"Take over the phone, Hughie," Jolly said to the man. "I don't expect there'll be much. Mind you don't let anybody come in too late on the three-thirty."

The man nodded and rose to his feet. Jolly closed the door of the hut and stepped away from it.

"If Dessie isn't at home this minute," he said, "you'd better not be seen talking to me."

His gaze did not waver when Martineau looked at him. The policeman asked: "Do you know something I don't know?"

Jolly grunted an affirmative. He lit a cigarette and left it in the corner of his mouth.

"She should be home by three o'clock," he said. "It's well turned three now. Happen she'll be a bit late, or happen she won't come at all. Happen I'm just a mug."

"Tell me more," said Martineau.

Jolly glanced at Cassidy, and at the passers-by in Wales Road. "Come round to the back," he said.

They went to the rear of the hut, where there was just enough space for a small man to swing a cat. Jolly took an envelope from his pocket. "Happen I shouldn't do this," he said. "I might be putting Dessie in danger."

He handed the envelope to Martineau, who turned it over and read the inscription: "SAM JOLLY ESQ." It was a cheap white paper envelope of postcard size. There was no stamp, and no postmark.

"Hughie found it shoved through the letter box here when he came to work," said Jolly.

Martineau took a sheet of plain stationery from the envelope. He unfolded it and read it through. "A ransom note, by God!" he breathed. He was astounded. In all his twenty years of police service he had never seen a ransom note. Nor did he know any other policeman who had seen one. This sort of thing did not happen in England. It might happen in America, or in Sicily or even in Ireland, but not in England.

Martineau read the note again. It was written in block letters, in ink.

IF YOU WANT D.K. ALIVE AND UNHARMED PUT 50 POUND IN USED POUND NOTES IN A WHITE ENVELOPE AND LEAVE IT BEFORE 2 O'CLOCK TODAY INSIDE TOP WALL OF BURNSIDE PARK BEHIND THE TREES ON THAT LITTLE HILL. DO THIS AND D.K. WILL BE HOME SAFE AND SOUND BY 3. IF YOU TELL POLICE OR TRY ANY TRICKS YOULL BE SORRY. SORRY FOR THE KID YOULL BE. REMEMBER YOULL BE WATCHED.

"Fifty quid," said Martineau in disgust. "Would you credit it? What did you do about it?"

"I did what the note told me to do," said Jolly steadily. "Where little Dessie's safety is concerned, fifty quid is neither here nor there. I suspected I was being taken for a mug, but I gambled the fifty in the hope that there might be some truth in the note. Whoever wrote it is crackers, and folk who are crackers are liable to do anything."

"What do you mean by 'crackers'? Insane?"

"Just plain daft, more like. Somebody who's been reading about kidnapers in America, or seen it at the pictures. Somebody daft enough to try it on here for a miserable fifty. And happen daft enough to hurt the child if I refused to pay."

"Well, we'd better find out if the child has arrived home. Then we'll see if the ransom money has been taken. Did you see anybody watching when you planted it?"

"No. It was half-past one and there was nobody about."

"M'm. Well, let's go."

"You go ahead, I'll follow. I still prefer to play it safe."

"Just as you like. I shall want you to show me the place in the park where you left the money."

"It's easy enough to find. I'd rather you watched it from a distance."

"A bit late in the day for you to suggest that, isn't it? If you had reported this matter as soon as you got the note, we could have watched the place through field glasses without the slightest danger to the child. By this time we would have had the man who wrote the note, and Dessie as well, *if* he knows where she is."

Jolly was unconvinced. "If I'd told you about it, you'd have had so many coppers on the job he'd have spotted something. You'd have been more keen on getting the man. I was only interested in the child."

The suggestion by an untrained civilian that the Granchester C.I.D. could not handle a simple job of observation made Martineau's eyes glint. But Jolly's appearance of absolute integrity restrained him. Evidently the man had done the right thing according to his way of thinking. He could not be expected to view the matter as a policeman would.

"I found time to write down the numbers of all the notes," said Jolly.

"Did you, begad? That might be a help. Where's the list?"

The bookmaker took two folded sheets of paper from an inside pocket. "Things have been a bit slack today, so I made a copy later on, just in case."

"Which is the copy?"

"This one."

"I'll take it. I'll receipt it with time and date, and then you can put your name on it. I'll sign your list, then I can swear it's the original list you showed me."

This was done, and the papers tucked away. Martineau said: "See you at the house," and departed.

He took Cassidy with him. He wondered briefly what had happened to Devery, but forgot about him when he saw a police pillar. He phoned Headquarters, and told Clay about the ransom note.

"And where are you going now?" Clay wanted to know.

"I'm going to the house to see if the kid has turned up."

"Some hopes you've got," was the rough-voiced comment. "That note sounds like a fake to me. All right, keep in touch."

Martineau went on his way, and thought about Jolly. He had seen the bookmaker take a big wad of notes from a cashbox and pocket them, *before* he was supposed to know anything about a ransom note. But that was not a definite indication of either collusion or subterfuge. Racing men invariably carried a lot of money, when they had money.

At the house in Mold Street, Mrs. Kegan was sitting alone.

"Anything new?" Martineau asked.

She shook her head. "Nothing at all," she answered sadly. "Have you any news?"

"I'm afraid not," he replied gently. "But don't give up. It hasn't been twenty-four hours yet."

They talked about the case for a few minutes. It seemed to relieve the woman to repeat what Mrs. So-and-so thought, and what little Mary Whatshername had said. Then Jolly arrived. There was no need for Martineau to say anything. Jolly did not show the disappointment he was supposed to feel. With kindness and affection he asked Mrs. Kegan how she was. She told him that she was a bundle of nerves. He advised her to go and lie down, and said that he would bring her tea and aspirins shortly. Meekly but with obvious reluctance she went upstairs.

Martineau looked at his watch. Jolly noticed the movement, and said: "There's still time for Dessie to turn up."

"Have you some hope?" the detective asked drily.

"No, not really," came the admission. "I guess I've been done for fifty. Well, it was worth a try."

"We might find your fifty. The fellow might start flashing his wad."

Jolly shrugged. "Find us the kid," he said.

Martineau thought regretfully about what could have been done if Jolly had passed the ransom note to the police as soon as he had received it. The delivery and collection of the fifty pounds could have been observed by officers standing well back from an upstairs window of one of the shops in Wales Road. Prior to that, the money could have been treated with eosin or Rhodamine B, so that the self-styled kidnaper's takings, his hands, his wallet and his pocket, in ordinary circumstances apparently unmarked, would have fluoresced vividly under the dark rays of the ultraviolet lamp. But there was no point in lecturing the bookmaker about that. The thing was done.

"We'll keep all policemen away from the park for a while, at any rate," he said. "But you can go into the park. With the child not delivered on time, it will be the most natural thing in the world for you to go and see if the money has been collected. If it *hasn't* been collected, leave it where it is."

"I'll do that," said Jolly. "It'll be a slight relief to know."

"I'll wait here for you. Don't trample around any more than you can help, and don't touch anything."

"Right," the man said. He went out. Martineau and Cassidy settled down to wait. "I think we have time for a smoke," the senior officer said. They both lit cigarettes.

Twelve minutes later, by Martineau's watch, Jolly returned. "There's a torn white envelope, and it looks like the one I put the money in," he said. "The money was gone."

Martineau rose. "I think we'd better start work on it," he said. "We may find something."

A car stopped outside. A door slammed. There was a knock on the open door of the house. Jolly turned to look. "I think it will be somebody for you," he said.

Martineau went to the door. There was a uniformed motor-patrol officer. "Chief Superintendent Clay would like to speak to you, sir," he announced. "He's receiving now."

The chief inspector went to the car, and slid into the seat beside the driver. "Martineau here," he said, and then he turned over to reception.

Clay spoke to him. "I've got news for you. Sergeant Devery reports that he saw Albert Vizard come out of Burnside Park at five minutes to three, walking on the tips of his toes with his hat on the side of his head, if you know what I mean. He got the impression that Vizard had just done something. Vizard took a taxi to Granchester Public Library and went into the reference room. He consulted lawbooks, and he was not seen to dump anything. Now he's on his way back to Burnside, with Devery on his tail. You had better stand by until I hear from Devery again. Over."

"I'll stand by, sir," said Martineau, controlling his pleased excitement. "I'll be waiting on receive."

Fifteen minutes later Clay spoke again. "I've heard from Sergeant Devery. Vizard has gone home. Devery is watching the house with the help of a civilian. I'm rushing a search warrant out there, to Flint Street I mean. Make your way circumspectly and contact Devery. Over."

"I'm on my way," said Martineau.

He instructed the driver of the police car to wait or cruise about in Wales Road, ready for a call. Then he and Cassidy set off to walk the short distance to Flint Street. Jolly gazed after them as they went away, then he shook his head and stepped indoors.

As they approached the vicinity of Vizard's home, the two detectives kept a sharp lookout for Devery, whom they did not expect to see standing in plain view. They did not find him, but Cassidy drew Martineau's attention to a man who was signaling to them from the interior of an ivory-colored Ford car.

"That'll be the civvy who's helping Devery," said Martineau. "I'd better not walk across to him, I'm too well known to Vizard. Go and see what he has to say."

Cassidy went, and returned. "A man called Campbell, sir," he reported. "He's watching the front, and Sergeant Devery is round the back. He says a stout woman left the house about five minutes after Vizard entered. She was carrying a shopping basket. Then a few minutes later a younger woman arrived and went in."

"The stout woman would be Vizard's sister. I hope she wasn't carrying anything for him. We'll have to wait and see who the other woman is. Now you go round to the back and relieve Sergeant Devery. Send him to me."

When Devery arrived, Martineau received a full account of Vizard's activities. In return, he told Devery about the ransom note.

"So we really are on to something," was the sergeant's comment. "I'm glad it's a money job. I couldn't figure it out, and I was half afraid we were going to hear that another little girl was missing."

"I wish they'd be quick with that warrant," said Martineau.

The warrant arrived when they had waited twenty minutes. It was in the hands of Detective Constable Ducklin, who came in a small C.I.D. car. "The Guv'nor sent the keys as well, sir," he said. "He thought you might want to go in quick and quiet."

The "keys" were on a wire ring as big as a horse collar. They were an assortment of hundreds of master keys which the C.I.D. had collected over a period of years. Some officers were very skillful in examining a lock and selecting a key which would open it. Devery was one of these. He had always been interested in locks.

"You had better go and give our thanks to your friend Mr. Campbell, and tell him he's at liberty," said Martineau. "Then we'll get on with the job."

Devery obeyed the order, and Campbell drove away with a cheerful wave of his hand. Then the three policemen walked quickly toward the Vizard home, with Devery carrying the ring of keys under his coat. If the door of the house had to be unlocked, his own body and those of his companions would screen his activities from the inquisitive eyes of neighbors. He knew quite well what Clay had meant when he had suggested that the entry of the police might have to be quick and quiet. Fifty pounds was not an enormous amount of paper money. It could soon be burned. If made into small bundles by a frightened criminal, it could soon be washed away down a water closet and lost forever.

Their entry was quicker and quieter than they had expected. The door was not locked. Martineau tried it, and it opened silently. He led the way into the house. He looked around, and found that the living room and the kitchen were deserted. He listened for a moment at the foot of the stairs, and heard nothing. Carefully he began to climb. A stair creaked loudly under his not inconsiderable weight, so he went up at a run, with the others at his heels. He opened the door of Albert Vizard's bedroom and looked in. Two startled faces stared at him from the pillow of Vizard's bed. Mr. and Mrs. Vizard had, apparently, resumed conjugal relations.

10.

AT Headquarters, Rosa Vizard was put in Martineau's office under the care of a policewoman, while Albert Vizard was taken to the charge room and searched. In his pockets he had fifty-three one-pound notes and some change. Fifty of the notes were wadded in an inside pocket. Martineau compared their numbers with those which Jolly had given him, ticking them off on the list one by one.

"Correct," he said. He looked at Vizard, who was watching him apprehensively. "I'm not going to ask you where you got this money. I know. What you *are* going to tell me is—where is Dessie Kegan?"

"I don't know. I know nothing about her."

"What did you do with her?"

"Nothing. I never touched her."

"Then what made you start sending ransom notes?"

"I was hard up. It was a chance to make some spending money. I guessed one or the other of 'em would pay."

Martineau did not show his surprise. He reflected that his own mention of ransom notes in the plural was a fortunate accident. He also realized that his next question would have to be very carefully phrased to give Vizard the impression that the police knew everything about the matter in hand.

"You knew Sam Jolly *could* pay. But what about the other one?"

"He could pay an' all. He's been saving up for a court case to get the kid away from his wife. He won't need to bother about that now."

So, the detective thought, John Kegan had been sent a ransom note, too. "Why won't he need to bother?" he asked.

"Well, summat must have happened to her. Anybody can see that."

"Anybody who knows. What did you do with her?"

Vizard did not seem to be alarmed by the repetition of a question which was virtually an accusation of murder. "I never laid a finger on her," he said.

"You won't get away with that. You knew she wouldn't be found by three o'clock this afternoon. That's why you thought you could take a chance on trying to rob her father of all he had."

"He robbed me of my wife, didn't he? He did it while I was in the mental home, too."

"But he didn't let you rob him, did he? He didn't pay."

"No, he didn't. Him what reckons to dote on the kid. Happen he could see no sense in paying. Happen he's the one who knows where she is."

"How do you know he received your note?"

Vizard shrugged. "I posted it last night. He should have got it first thing this morning."

"What address?"

"Eleven Collier Street. I used to live there, remember. Don't *you* know whether he got it or not?"

"I'm not here to tell you what I know," said Martineau. "Didn't your wife tell you whether or not he had received the note?"

"No. I never asked her. She knows nothing about it."

"Then why did she meet you this afternoon?"

"I'll let you guess about that. She's still my wife, you know. We never even bothered to get a legal separation."

Martineau was silent, staring absently at the prisoner, thinking about him. Vizard was in deep trouble. The judge or recorder who would eventually give him his deserts would take a very poor view of his attempt to exploit a grievous situation, whether or not he had caused it. He did not seem to realize that. He seemed to be hardly aware of wrongdoing. At first he had been afraid, but not now. And with regard to the disappearance of Dessie Kegan, he seemed to be certain that nothing could be proved against him in connection with it. Why was this little sparrow of a man so sure of himself with regard to Dessie? Any man, even one so queer as Vizard, should have been worried by an accusation of child murder. What were the possibilities? Had he killed Dessie and disposed of her body so efficiently that he was positive it would never be found? Or was he one of those schizophrenic types, conveniently able to lose all remembrance of horrible deeds committed? Martineau frowned when he thought of that. Like nearly all policemen, he had strong views about this new thing, diminished responsibility. He did not like to see criminals evading punishment by being, or pretending to be, crackers.

"Take him to the grillroom and get a clerk," he said to Cassidy. "Wait for me there."

He left the charge room then, and went to his own office. Rosa Vizard was sitting in a chair which faced the window, while the policewoman was sitting on a chair beside the door. The chief inspector took the seat at his desk, so that he faced Rosa and had his back to the policewoman.

"Now, Mrs. Vizard," he said. "Sorry to keep you waiting. This is a bad affair."

"Why have I been brought here?" she wanted to know. Her manner was somewhat truculent, but he perceived that she was afraid of something.

"That's a reasonable question," he said. "You were brought here for interrogation, because you were found in the company of your husband soon after he had committed a crime. In other words, I want to find out if you were involved."

"What do you mean, involved? Involved in what?"

"Involved in the crime."

Her voice was contemptuous. "What crime could *he* commit?"

"The murder of Dessie Kegan, perhaps."

She caught her breath. "Is that why you arrested him? Have they found her?"

Martineau studied her, trying to guess what was in her mind. He did not answer her questions, but asked: "Are you trying to tell me that you have no idea why your husband was arrested?"

"I've been trying to tell you for some time. What has he done?"

"If you're not involved, having no knowledge of any crime, there is no need for me to tell you, yet."

"And having no knowledge of any crime, there's no need for you to keep me here."

"Well taken," he said, with a slight smile. "Just a few more questions, and then I might let you go. This afternoon, did you meet Albert by appointment?"

She hesitated. "Yes," she said.

"When was the appointment made?"

"What has that got to do with you? It's no business of yours."

"It might be. What day was it?"

"One day during the week. I don't remember which."

"Was it Friday?"

"No. No, it wasn't Friday. It may have been Wednesday. I'm not sure."

"What time of day was it?"

"I don't remember."

"Morning, afternoon or evening?"

"I don't remember. What does it matter, anyway?"

"It matters because I find it strange that you should meet your husband in secret. Are you thinking of taking him back to live with you?"

"I might be."

"Somehow I find that hard to believe. Did he promise you money if you would meet him?"

"Well, really!"

"Did he?"

"He did not!"

"You say the appointment was not made on Friday. Did you see him at all on Friday?"

"No."

"H'm. What time did you get up today?"

"Oh, hell, what next? Eight o'clock."

"What time did Kegan get up?"

"About ten."

"You caught the post, then?"

"What post? There was no post."

"Wasn't there a letter delivered at your house this morning?"

"I never saw any letter."

"H'm," said Martineau. "All right, you may go. I expect Kegan will still be snoring. Where did you leave the child?"

"Next door."

"I see." Martineau turned to the policewoman. "Will you see Mrs. Vizard off the premises?"

"Just a minute," said Rosa. "Aren't you going to tell me why Albert has been locked up?"

"He was locked up because he had a pocketful of somebody else's money."

Rosa's eyes widened. It seemed that she now understood something which had been a puzzle to her. But she said: "Well, I didn't get any of it. He didn't give me a cent."

Martineau nodded his acceptance of that statement. He said: "All right," and rose from his chair.

She said: "Wait," and now her fear was naked in her eyes. Martineau waited, and she said: "Will you tell Jack—Mr. Kegan—about seeing me with Albert?"

"Wouldn't you like that?"

"No, I wouldn't!"

"I see," said Martineau. "You don't want to quarrel with Kegan. Not in that way, at any rate. Of course I won't say anything to him *unless* some unforeseen development compels me to."

"Don't tell him, please!"

"I have told you I won't, except under compulsion. That's the best I can do. Now off you go."

She went, escorted by the policewoman. Martineau stood in thought, staring at the brown linoleum on his office floor. There was a knock on the door, and Devery looked in. "We searched the house, sir," he reported. "Nothing at all. I waited until his sister returned and informed her of Vizard's arrest. I got the clothes he was wearing yesterday and sent Ducklin to the laboratory with them."

Martineau nodded, and Devery asked: "What now, sir?"

"I've got him in the grillroom. You had better come along. This afternoon's lark will probably be your case."

The Interrogation Room, also called the grillroom, the steam-room, and the bank manager's office, was admirably constructed for the purpose of applying psychological pressure, which is the only kind of pressure which the British police are allowed to exert as inquisitors. It was a large, windowless room, gray-walled, concrete-floored, with one central table and two chairs, and a smaller table and a chair in a corner. The corner table had a small, hooded light, but a single large bulb was suspended above the center table. This central light was shaded so that strong illumination beat down upon the table, while the walls and corners of the room were shadowed. This sinister effect was quite unplanned, but nevertheless it was appreciated by police officers. The gray walls had originally been intended as a setting for white tiles. A washroom it should have been. For some reason during construction, work upon it had been postponed, and the C.I.D. had found it useful for other purposes. After a while its value had been recognized, and the openings left for the plumbers had been filled in and smoothed over.

In the Interrogation Room, when Martineau knocked for admission, were Vizard seated at a center table, Cassidy standing with his back to the door, and a C.I.D. clerk seated at the small table in the corner. When he heard the knock, Cassidy noisily shot back a large bolt, then he unlocked the door and pulled it open as if it were made of solid lead. When Martineau and Devery had entered, the big Irishman slammed the door, turned the key, shot the bolt, and then put his back to the door and stood with folded arms. It was all part of the business, done for the public benefit, to make enemies of the public feel that they were in a place where any dreadful thing might happen to them. Occasionally, mistakenly, that feeling was imposed upon people who were quite innocent of any offense. That was to be expected, since no policeman is infallible. But it is fair to say that such mistakes were rarely made.

Martineau took the chair across the table from Vizard's, and sat looking at him for a long moment. It was obvious to him that the waiting treatment, in that room, had had some effect on the prisoner. The man's eyes were wild with apprehension now. He had had time to realize that he really was in trouble, and he was afraid of what might happen to him in that room. All the rumors he had ever heard about "third degree" would now be uppermost in his mind.

The chief inspector lit a cigarette. He blew smoke at the overhead light. He remained silent, at ease, apparently quite contented.

"For God's sake give me a cigarette," said Vizard.

"You don't smoke."

"Give me a couple of aspirins, then. I have a headache."

Martineau turned his head. "Anybody got any aspirins?"

Nobody moved or spoke. Martineau said: "Sorry, no aspirins. You don't find drugs of any kind in a police station."

Vizard locked his fingers and pressed his hands together. "What are we waiting for?" he burst out.

"We're waiting for the truth. The whole truth."

"I told you the truth."

"Why did you go to the library?"

"To consult a reference book."

"With regard to what?"

"It was a medical book. I'm interested in diseases of the nerves."

"That's a lie," said Martineau, suddenly harsh and menacing.

Vizard's eyes flickered. He looked about, as if he sought a way of escape. "Don't you dare touch me," he shrilled. "I'm delicate. I show every bruise. If you lay a hand on me my doctor will get you all sacked."

"You consulted some lawbooks. What was it you wanted to know?"

Vizard was silent.

"Ask me," urged Martineau, grimly jovial. "I know something about law. I may be able to answer your question. All these fellows here know something about law. *They* may be able to answer your question."

"It—it was a private matter."

"It is sometimes necessary for the police to inquire about private matters. What was it?"

"It was something about me and my wife."

"Be more explicit."

Vizard became hysterical. He also wept. "I won't tell you! I won't! I won't!" he cried.

Martineau sat back and waited. Vizard could not shed tears forever. Without being spoken to either in sympathy or antipathy, he could only remain hysterical for a limited time.

The wild weeping subsided. Vizard gasped, sobbed and sniffled. He wiped his eyes with the soiled handkerchief which was the only personal possession which the police had allowed him to retain. He blew his nose, then his glance met Martineau's.

That was what the policeman had been waiting for. He spoke at once, but to calm the man he repeated his questions of yesterday, concerning Vizard's movements on that day. Vizard's efforts to remember, and to give substantially the same answers, seemed to act like a sedative. In a little while he was speaking quite normally.

Then Martineau returned to the attack. "I'm going to touch on your private affairs, and with reason," he said. "Did you meet your wife by appointment this afternoon?"

The suspect thought before he answered. "Yes."

"When was the appointment made?"

"Er . . . Thursday, I think."

"That isn't what your wife said."

"What did she say?"

"I won't tell you just what she said, but didn't you meet her on Friday?"

"No," came the immediate reply. "I never saw her at all on Friday."

"H'm. You're sure it was Thursday?"

"No, I'm not at all sure. It may have been Wednesday."

"Morning or afternoon?"

"I just forget. I just met her casual, like."

"Where?"

"Er . . . Wales Road."

Martineau appeared to be satisfied with that answer. He turned abruptly to the subject of Dessie Kegan. "You did see Dessie on Friday, didn't you?" he suggested.

"No. I told you. I never did."

The policeman pressed him, putting his questions in various ways, trying to trap him into making a damaging admission. He made no headway. Vizard was calm, strangely unworried. Obviously he knew, or thought he knew, that in the matter of Dessie Kegan he was quite safe.

Eventually Martineau could find no more angles from which to shoot the same old questions. Nevertheless, he was not dissatisfied. In a negative way, he had learned enough to form a theory. He began to clear up odd points.

"Fifty pounds is a very small sum for the ransom of a human being," he said. "Why only fifty?"

"Kegan couldn't raise more than fifty, even if he borrowed," said Vizard frankly, willing to talk now that the subject was changed.

"But Jolly could."

"Jolly is no relation to the kid. And he's shrewd. I thought he might not spring more than fifty."

"When did you deliver Jolly's letter?"

"I shoved it through his letter box Friday night. Half-past ten, happen."

"We know about your instructions to Jolly. Where did you tell Kegan to leave his money?"

"Behind the summerhouse near the far wall of the park."

"In a white envelope?"

"Yes. Look here, didn't you know about Kegan's letter?"

"No. You told me about it."

Vizard swore. He pondered. "Ah, well," he said wearily. "You'd happen have got to know, anyway. Can I lie down somewhere? I'm absolutely done in."

"Yes, you can lie down. The clerk will put what you have said into the form of a statement, then you can sign it."

"You can't force me to sign anything. I'm not signing nothing."

"As you wish," said Martineau indifferently. He glanced at Devery. "Get him charged, then take him down and lock him up," he said. "Then get on the phone and ask the police surgeon to have a look at him. That way he won't be able to make any complaints about his treatment here."

11.

WHEN Albert Vizard had been taken to the cells, Martineau told Devery to order a car while he went to report to Chief Superintendent Clay.

He told his story, and concluded: "So we're no nearer to the child."

The chief of the C.I.D. was grimly sarcastic. "And are you satisfied with your efforts?" he wanted to know.

"Not quite. There's something damned funny about Vizard. He's as confident as hell when I touch on the subject of Dessie. He knows something, but he won't put it to music. I'd like to sweat it out of him, but he's such a weakling I hardly dare raise my voice."

"Well, we're not going to let him get away with anything. He's as likely a suspect as we've come across yet. I'll have a go at him myself as soon as the notes of the interview have been transcribed. What are you going to do now?"

"I want to know something about the second ransom letter. If Kegan received it, it's strange that he did nothing about it. You'd think he would have done *something*, wouldn't you?"

"Yes. It's strange as you say. But how is it going to get us nearer to the child?"

Martineau permitted himself a grin. "You used to tell me to explore every avenue, leave no stone unturned, take nothing for granted, suspect everybody, and don't trust the Archbishop of Canterbury's daughter."

"So I did," Clay admitted with a wry smile. "All right. You *might* turn something up. At least you'll be in a good position to go ahead with the job when it breaks."

"When we find the body, you mean?" said Martineau, his grin fading.

"I'm afraid that's what it will be," Clay answered with a sigh. "I can hardly believe the kid is still alive."

"Well, we can only keep bashing on. I'll be off."

"Wait a minute. That reminds me. I don't like putting on good nature, but the men who are watching Clare and Barker are dying on their feet. They've been at it all night and all day, and I haven't a suitable relief for them. If I find you a few men, can you and Sergeant Devery take over the job at ten o'clock tonight, until two? That will allow you an hour or two's rest this evening, maybe."

"I'll do that, sir. Something might happen tonight. At ten o'clock I'll be on the job."

"Thank you," said Clay.

Martineau went out of the building, trying to remember how many years it was since Clay had last uttered thanks to a subordinate. He found Devery waiting at the wheel of a plain car. They went to Mold Street first, where he drew Sam Jolly to one side and told him that the whole of his money had been recovered.

The bookmaker was surprised. "My word, you've been quick," he said.

"The good luck and alertness of my colleague here."

"Who was it?"

Martineau realized that for his own purposes he might have to give the information to Kegan. So there was no point in keeping it from Jolly. "Albert Vizard," he said.

"What about Dessie? Did he have her?"

"We don't know yet. We'll keep at him, of course. Now I must be going. Cheerio."

"So long, Inspector. Anything I can do, let me know."

"Where now?" Devery asked, when they were in the car. "Kegan's place?"

"Not yet. I think we'll try and establish proof of delivery first.

The local postman may actually remember putting the ransom note through Kegan's letter box."

Devery grimaced. Of all official organizations in Britain the G.P.O., through its personnel, is perhaps the most reluctant to give information to the police. No doubt this unwillingness arises from the tradition of the inviolable privacy of the Royal Mail, but the police do not perceive any of that. They mutter about hidebound officiousness and willful obstruction.

"Do I drive to the G.P.O., then?"

"You do not," said Martineau. "They'd have to write to the Postmaster General before they could tell us the postman's name. I think we'll do better at the subpost office in Wales Road."

The visit to the post office and the subsequent trip to a postman's house in Dadsbury took up an hour of their time. Their journey was rewarded by the postman's positive statement that he had delivered a letter to John Kegan, 11 Collier Street, that morning. He remembered the letter because he had seen in a morning paper that John Kegan was the father of Dessie Kegan.

They left the postman, and returned to their car.

"Now we'll go and see if Kegan has sobered up," said Martineau. "If we get the letter, we get more evidence against Vizard. If we don't get the letter, we might get some information indirectly, through the heated words which will be spoken."

"I don't think we'll see any letter," said Devery.

"Neither do I," came the rejoinder. "We might see nothing at all, but at least we'll complete the inquiry."

Collier Street was quiet. There were no women at their doors, and there were no children playing. For this was Saturday night, when even the poorest and most thrifty felt that they could afford a visit to a cinema or a public house.

The door of No. 11 was closed. Martineau knocked. After a little while the knock was answered by Kegan himself. His swarthy face was haggard, but he was sober, and newly washed and shaved. Evidently he was ready to go out again.

His face lighted with the expression of mingled hope and uncertainty which the detectives were beginning to know only too well. "You've found her?" he asked.

"No, I'm sorry to say," Martineau replied. "But I want to see you about a little matter connected with her. May we come in?"

"Oh, sure," said Kegan, his face falling into somber lines. He held open the door for them.

They entered. There was no one else in the room. "Is Mrs. Vizard out?" the chief inspector asked.

"She's upstairs, putting the baby to bed," Kegan answered curtly. "What did you want to see me about?"

"Did you receive a letter this morning, through the post?"

"No. I received no letter."

"A letter was delivered here."

"Well, I never saw it. Rosa might know something about it. I'll ask her when she comes downstairs. She's just putting the baby to bed."

"We'll wait, then, if you don't mind."

"Sure. What was this letter? How do you know it was delivered here?"

"I talked to the man who sent it, and to the postman who delivered it."

"It sounds important. What was it?"

"A ransom note."

"A ransom note?" Kegan was astounded. "Do you mean to say somebody has kidnaped Dessie?"

"I believe that was the information in the letter. There were two, you see. One was sent to you, one to another person. Fifty pounds was the sum mentioned in each letter."

"A lousy fifty pounds for my kid? How do you know all this? Have you nabbed the man who sent the letters?"

"Yes."

"And you haven't got Dessie yet? Can't you make him tell?

Can't you wring it out of him? Let me see him. I'll make him talk."

"We're doing our best with him, but he says he knows nothing about the child. We can't get more than that out of him—yet. He says he just moved in to make a small profit out of the job."

"Who is this great guy?"

Martineau appeared to hesitate. He seemed to consider. Then he said: "Albert Vizard is the man."

"That little rat! I should have known! He's done something to Dessie just to spite me. Wait till I get my hands on him!"

"It'll be rather a long wait, I'm afraid. He's in plenty of trouble."

Hatred of the man he had wronged blazed in Kegan's eyes. "I'm right glad to hear it," he said. "Are you wanting this ransom letter for evidence?"

"That's right."

Kegan became calmer. His eyes narrowed thoughtfully. "If I bother Rosa now, I'll disturb the baby," he said. "She should be down any minute."

Martineau had a shrewd idea that Rosa was listening at the head of the stairs, but he made no comment. He estimated that she would allow a minute or two to pass after the talk had ceased.

The three men waited in silence for a little while, then Rosa came down the stairs. Though hatless, she was dressed for the street. She was undoubtedly attractive in a casual coat and smart shoes, though the coat was by no means new.

Kegan challenged her immediately. "You were up first this morning. What did you do with my letter?"

Rosa's acting was superb. "What letter?" she asked indifferently. "I saw no letter."

"You must have done. The letter was delivered."

"Some kid must have pulled it out of the letter box before I came downstairs."

Kegan looked at Martineau. The detective shook his head.

"That's a point I asked about," he said. "The letter was pushed properly through the slot. None of it was left sticking out."

"There you are," said Kegan. "Come on, where is it?"

"I tell you I never saw any letter," Rosa answered with contempt. "Baby was crawling about. He might have found it and chucked it away somewhere. He might even have chewed it up. What was it, a summons or summat?"

Kegan went to the door, and started a search. The moment his back was turned, Rosa's glance sought Martineau's face. Her fear was revealed to him then. Her eyes implored him to remain silent about the events of the afternoon. His level gaze did not change. He left her with no clue to his intentions.

Kegan looked beneath every article of furniture in the room. Then he went to the fireplace, which contained ash and cold cinders from the last fire which had burned there. He found nothing in the fireplace. If the letter had been burned, the charred remains had been thoroughly broken up. He opened a shallow drawer in the sideboard. The contents indicated that it was Rosa's personal drawer. He rummaged about, then closed the drawer with a bang.

"Where is it?" he demanded, beside himself. "Where is that letter?"

"*I* don't know where the damned letter is," she retorted, toughly unmoved again. "What's so important about it, anyway?"

"It's evidence against your perishing husband, that's what it is. And you're concealing it. Did you know it was from him?"

"Oh, blast you," she said. "For the last time, I never saw any letter."

"You're lying."

Rosa looked with disdain at the father of her child. "I'm going out," she said.

She picked up a pair of gloves from the sideboard and pulled them on forcibly, as if she were at the end of her patience. To do this she had to put down her small handbag of pale leather,

which she had been holding down by her side. As she picked up
the handbag, Kegan moved between her and the door. "Give me
that bag," he said, quietly resolute now.

"What right have you in a lady's handbag?" she wanted to
know.

"Give it me."

She gave it to him. He opened it and emptied its contents on
to the table. There were cigarettes and matches, a tiny purse, a
mirror, a handkerchief, and the usual jumble of cosmetics. He
felt around the lining of the bag. He opened the purse. Then he
replaced everything and returned the bag to her.

"Satisfied?" she asked coldly.

"No," he said.

She turned away. As she did so she gave Martineau a baffling
glance which seemed to him to hold both a prayer and a promise.
"You be good to me, and I'll be good to you," she seemed to say.
With that last instinctive attempt to ensure Martineau's silence
she was gone, and the door was left wide-open.

"If that letter is in the house I'll find it in the morning," said
Kegan, as the sound of Rosa's heels faded along the street. "I'll
give it to you for evidence. By the way, who got the other letter?"

"Jolly."

"Did he pay up?"

"Yes."

"H'm. I wouldn'ta thought it. Had Vizard spent any of it?"

"No."

"A pity," said Kegan.

After that, there was no point in lingering. The two detectives
left the house, and Kegan went out with them. He locked the
door, leaving the sleeping baby alone. The policemen looked at
each other.

"Oh, we're not as bad as all that," said Kegan, noticing the
exchange of glances. "Mrs. Dawson will be home from the pictures in a little while. She'll pop in and keep an eye on the bairn."

He dropped the key through the letter box of the house next door. "Can we give you a lift toward town?" Martineau asked.

"No fear," was the prompt reply. "I've got my reputation to think about. If folk see me riding with coppers they'll start getting funny ideas."

The car overtook and passed him as he walked along the street. He waved in friendly fashion. "He's on our side now," said Devery.

"So long as he thinks he's helping us to tread on Vizard's neck," Martineau replied.

Rosa Vizard was not in sight in Eden Street. The car reached the junction with Wales Road, and turned the corner. Still Rosa was not in sight along the straight, sparsely peopled road. "That's funny," said Martineau. "She must have popped inside somewhere. Stop the car and we'll wait a minute."

While they waited, a tall young man in a good gray suit walked past the car and looked at them curiously. Martineau recognized him. He lowered the window of the car, and called: "Oy!"

The young man, who was P.C. 942 Vincent, stopped and turned. "Sir," he said.

"You've done your twelve hours today, haven't you?" the chief inspector queried. "What are you doing around here? You should be in town having a well-earned pint with a few of the lads."

"To tell you the truth, sir, I'm unofficially on duty," Vincent replied candidly. "I want to get into this thing if I can. Is there anything you'd like me to do?"

"Yes, in a moment. Get in the car."

Vincent did as he was bidden. Martineau turned to look out of the rear window. "Get down, Vincent, right down," he said, "and come up quick when I tell you."

Vincent disappeared from view. Kegan passed. The two men in the front seat of the car were apparently peering at a map by the light from the dashboard.

"Up," said Martineau. "Take a look at that fellow going away from us. That's John Kegan, father of Dessie Kegan. He lives with the girl you'll be following, when she shows up. If she doesn't show up, you'll have to follow him."

Kegan went straight along the road, without looking back. He passed a public house called the Rook Inn. After he had passed, someone could be seen peeping round the corner of the inn doorway. "That's our Rosa, for a pound," said Devery.

The time of day was now approaching eight o'clock, and the sky was quite dark, but under the sodium lights of Wales Road Rosa was easily recognizable as she stepped out of the inn doorway. She set off in the same direction as Kegan, a good hundred yards behind him.

"Trickle along after her," ordered Martineau. And then, almost jocularly: "I don't think there's anything more in this than a bit of honest cheating."

The car slowly followed Rosa, and Kegan could be seen ahead of her. Soon Kegan was crossing the road, making for the Flying Dutchman. He entered the inn.

Rosa did not follow Kegan. She looked at the Flying Dutchman as she passed, but went on toward the center of town. She walked only a few hundred yards further, to a big, modern gin palace called the Devonshire Arms. They watched her walk across the floodlit forecourt and enter by a door whose neon sign gave the information: "BAR LOUNGE."

"Good," said Martineau. He turned his head slightly to speak to Vincent. "Off you go. Make a note in the approved fashion of everything she does between now and hometime. Your job should be easier in a place like that. Don't get drunk."

Vincent grinned and got out of the car. They waited until he had passed under the neon sign.

Martineau lit a cigarette, and inhaled with audible pleasure. "I think that's all we can do about Dessie Kegan for today," he said. "Comes the night, and we turn our attention to Guy Rainer."

12.

GUY Rainer found that it was not so easy as he had imagined, to climb fifty feet inside a chimney by bracing his back against one side and his feet against the other. The chimney had been recently swept, and the soot which remained seemed greasy to his sweating hands. Occasionally he slipped downward a few inches when he was trying to ease himself upward. These heart-stopping incidents brought to his mind vivid pictures of himself hurtling down to the chimney bottom, and lying there undiscovered until he was long dead and unrecognizably carbonized. This fear exhausted him almost as much as the climb. When he finally got to the top of the chimney he was almost too weak to essay the tricky business of turning over in order to climb out. When eventually he did succeed in getting one leg over the edge he rested there for several minutes before he climbed out onto the roof.

The roof was not so steep as he had expected. He lay on his back and looked up at the stars, and rested. The stars, he thought, were glorious. How many million earthlings were there, he wondered, who almost never looked at the stars? Millions and millions and millions, he was sure. He remembered that he had not often looked at the stars himself before he was sent to prison, and had very seldom had the chance to look at them since. Once, on a ship in dock at night, a quartermaster had showed him the North Star and the most easily recognized constellations, but he had only been politely interested. In the near future, he reflected, he might be glad that he knew how to find the North Star. He looked for it now. He found it, then sat up and looked across the city. "Yes, that's north all right," he murmured, in agreement with the constant star.

The city's murky glow was like the reflection of hidden fires. Tall factories assumed queer cubistic shapes in the uncertain light. Huge cooling towers shone strange and gray. High chimney stacks, minarets of an obese golden god, were dimly visible. Babylon, he thought, industrial Babylon. Millions of its denizens had scratched for a living all the week in their million various ways, and now, on Saturday night, they were creeping about in the hazy glare on a million errands of pleasure. "Good old Granchester," he mused affectionately. "How the devil am I going to get away from you?"

He dared not stay on the roof too long, in case another search of the cellar resulted in the discovery of the open manhole. When he felt that he was fit for another climb he eased himself down the roof to the rain trough. He worked his way along the trough until he found the hole through which the trough emptied itself into the fall pipe. Firmly gripping the edge of the trough with both hands, he swung down from the roof and got a grip on the fall pipe with his knees. He transferred the grip of his hands to the pipe, and after that the descent was only hazardous in the matter of noise. In spite of the greatest care, his boots knocked the pipe a few times, making a soft, hollow sound which seemed terribly loud to him.

Then he was crouching on the flagstones of the schoolyard, at the rear of the school, looking to left and right as he rapidly unlaced his boots. He tied the boots to his belt. He took the short crowbar from the rule pocket of his boiler suit, and then he was ready for action. Tired though he was, without the heavy boots on his feet he had a feeling of lightness and swiftness.

He crept to a corner of the building and stood there listening. Round the corner, down some area steps, was the outer door of the basement. He felt sure that somebody would be watching that door to cover the possibility of his return to it. He reflected that there must be a very tight cordon round the neighborhood, for the police to be so sure that he was still in it. Well, cordons were made to be broken.

119

He continued to listen. He reasoned that no one could expect a policeman to wait all night long without making a sound. It wasn't possible. The man on guard, during his hours-long spell, must eventually clear his throat, or blow his nose, or make some movement which could be heard. The sentry invariably betrayed his presence and position to any marauder who could afford to listen long enough.

But in this case the sentry did not make a sound. It was, in a manner of speaking, the sergeant of the guard who pinpointed him for Guy. There was a low whistle, scarcely louder than a heavy sigh, a few yards away. Then the whispered reply could be heard.

"Pssst! I'm down here, Sarge."

"You all right?"

"Yes. Bloody fed up, that's all."

Guy guessed that the sergeant would be looking down into the area, where his subordinate lurked in deep shadow beside the basement door. He ventured to peep round the corner. In the starlight he saw a dim figure standing beside the area railings. The sergeant, he presumed. Would the sergeant go back, or would he decide to walk right round the building?

Guy did not wait for the answer to that question. He ran away from the corner, keeping close to the building, then he cut across the schoolyard toward an open shelter on the far side. He had to take the risk that there might be yet another policeman watching from the shelter.

He gained the shelter without hearing any sounds of alarm. No policeman was on guard there. He waited near the school wall, listening and staring across the yard. Before he could see anyone he heard the soft thump of rubber heels. The sergeant was coming to inspect the shelter. Without wasting any time Guy climbed the wall and dropped into St. Mary's churchyard.

In the churchyard he crawled round a grave so that he was hidden by the gravestone from anyone who might climb up and look over the school wall. He crouched there, listening hard and staring into the dark. The place was as quiet as the ancient dead who were in it. Not far away were the hedge and ditch which ran between the churchyard and the back gardens of the houses in Holly Road. The ditch, if it was not guarded, would take him to the perimeter wall of Holly Lodge. If he could not go by the ditch, he would have to crawl among gravestones until he reached the wall.

He was thankful for dry weather and warm airs. These were greater comforts to him than to his well-equipped enemies. Besides, a man left fewer traces of his passing in dry weather. Thinking of traces, he wondered when the police would begin to use dogs. Dogs were a danger which made him shudder. It did not occur to him that they had already been used.

He heard the sound of a passing vehicle in Holly Road, which never did carry a lot of traffic. He could also hear the distant hum of Wales Road, which was moderately busy even on Saturday night. He judged the time to be about ten o'clock. His knowledge of time tonight would never be more accurate than a guess. No church clock boomed in Burnside.

He began to crawl toward the ditch. He was in no hurry. He felt with his hands for twigs and small stones lying in his way, and carefully moved aside. So that it would not knock against anything, he stuck his crowbar into his belt at the back, between his boots.

Near the ditch he stopped to rest, listen and cautiously look around, and from his position on the ground he saw the heads and shoulders of two men in silhouette against the sky. They were standing beside the ditch, with their backs to it, halfway between his own position and the perimeter wall of Holly Lodge. He knew quite well why they had chosen that spot. The tall, untrimmed hedge was a dark background for them, and but for the circumstance that he was on their flank, close to the ground, he might not have seen them before they saw him. Standing thus in the most shadowy part of the churchyard, they were looking along the main, middle path toward the gate. And at the gate there was a street light. Anybody who crossed that path would be seen against the light. Even a cat would not get across undetected.

Guy breathed a few strong words. He was baffled. Neither the ditch nor the churchyard could be traversed while those men were there. Another way would have to be found. Somehow or other he had to get under cover before daylight. He had to get away from this place, through the grounds of Holly Lodge, and across Wales Road. How could he do that? Create a diversion? How could one man create a diversion without drawing attention to himself?

While he lay there trying to see a way out of the trap, he became aware of movement among the gravestones ahead of him. His first fear was that someone was stalking him; his second, that this was one of a line of policemen, searching among the graves. When he realized that it was no policeman, he sweated in apprehension that the careless fellow, whoever he might be, would draw police attention to this part of the churchyard. He wondered if it could be some drunk who had been lying asleep among the gravestones, or a man and a girl lying on the ground in seclusion.

As he peered in the unknown person's direction, he saw a head raised. It looked like the head of a man or a boy. He saw it duck and move as the man crawled toward the middle path. Guy thought that if he was a fugitive, his fate was sealed. Soon he would be crawling into the view of the men who stood by the ditch.

Guy was breathless with excitement; the sympathetic excitement of a man watching a trapeze artist. The moving head had gone out of sight, but he could still see the motionless heads of the two plain-clothes men. He did not shift his glance from them for several minutes. Then faintly a boot knocked against stone. He saw the two heads turn, and afterward remain immobile. In a little while the careless crawler made another sound, and the heads disappeared.

Whether or not the stranger made himself visible by trying to cross the path, Guy did not learn. But it became obvious to him that the two policemen had become sure of the man's presence, and had to some degree located him. His heart almost stopped beating as one of them came running lightly and furtively beside the ditch, straight toward the place where he lay. Alarm almost made him spring to his feet and reveal himself. But the man turned aside and dodged among gravestones, intent upon taking the stranger from the rear.

This move may have been perceived by the stranger. At any rate he sprang to his feet and fled. There was a shout and a rapid pounding of feet. Then there was silence. The unknown fugitive had gone to earth again.

A man spoke. There was the rasp of irritated authority in his voice. "Where is he? Did you see him?"

"He was somewhere just about here," came the anxious reply. Then: "He's there, going over the wall!"

"You stay here, where you can see the wall," the one in authority said. "I'll get the place sealed."

A police whistle was blown. The sound of it receded as the man who blew it went about his task of drawing policemen toward Holly Lodge. The men who heard the whistle would know what to do. It seemed unlikely that the stranger would escape them.

Guy slipped into the ditch, and made his way along it until he found a good hiding place in the hedge. His blackened face and dark, grimy clothes were invisible even from a few feet away. He crouched there for half an hour while the police surrounded Holly Lodge and searched it. He heard them crashing about inside the grounds, and saw the beams of their flashlights as they looked up into the trees. He heard the shout which meant that their quarry was sighted, and then the angry, frightened protest: "Let me go! I've done nowt!"

After that there seemed to be a general relaxation of police vigilance. Someone at the churchyard gate called: "Okay, we've got him," and men moved from among the graves. Guy assumed that they would also be leaving Holly Lodge. This was the time for him to move, before it was generally known among the policemen that the man they had arrested was not Guy Rainer.

He made his way to the perimeter wall of Holly Lodge. He stood close to the wall. He could see policemen standing in a group under the street lamp near the church gate. They appeared to be gossiping: one of them threw his head back and laughed at a colleague's comment. Guy moved along beside the wall, and went over it at a place nearly opposite the little glade with the broken fountain.

In the grounds all was still. He hoped that the police were no longer there, but he remembered his narrow escape on Friday night, and wondered if Martineau would try to trick him in the same way again. As he crossed the glade and went up the path which led to the house, he held his iron bar ready in his hand. But he met nobody. At the edge of the trees he halted. To the right, the lights of Holly Road showed him that the drive was deserted, and forward to the left he could see that nobody was standing at the front or side of the dark, silent house. Before him, on the other side of the drive, was a wide stretch of untended lawn with a belt of trees beyond. And through the trees twinkled the lights of Wales Road.

He crossed the drive, and when his unshod feet felt the cool, soft caress of the turf he began to run. He flitted along as dark and silent as an owl. There was no challenging shout or cry of warning. He gained the trees and went through them to the wall which abutted on Wales Road. The ground rose up to within two feet of the top of the wall, and an uncut privet hedge grew out over the sidewalk. He chose the darkest part of the hedge— furthest away from a street light—and crawled under it to look out at the world.

It was a normal fine Saturday night in Wales Road, with traffic passing at the rate of four or five vehicles in a minute. Looking to his left, Guy could see people emerging from a brightly lit

cinema three hundred yards away. To the right people loitered
at the crossroads a hundred yards away, and there was a queue
at the fish-and-chip shop just beyond. But there were no pedestrians where he was, where the long unbroken walls of Holly
Lodge and Markham's Mill faced each other.

He fixed his gaze on the crossroads. There, on the corner, two
tallish men in plain clothes and a policeman in uniform stood in
a group. Whatever they were talking about, it seemed to hold the
attention of all three. But one of them was facing in his direction, and that was enough to hold him motionless in concealment.

Time and traffic rolled by. A few people on foot passed close
to where Guy was hidden. The three policemen did not move
from the corner.

A double-decker bus came along, going toward Granchester.
Guy sank down until he was completely hidden by the wall. A
few seconds later, the scream of ill-treated tires startled him. He
raised his head. The bus had stopped at the crossroads, and its
slantwise position in relation to the curb suggested that it had
stopped very suddenly. In the middle of the crossing there was a
car, which also looked as if it had skidded a little way. The P.C.
in uniform was walking toward the car, possibly with the intention of admonishing the driver for the near accident. The two
plain-clothes men were watching the scene. All the loiterers at
the crossroads would be watching.

Guy craned to see more clearly. Traffic coming toward him
from Granchester was held at the crossing. One car traveling in
the other direction went by and stopped behind the bus. Except
for the people who were watching the P.C. and the car, there was
not a pedestrian within three hundred yards. It was Guy's chance.
He slid over the wall, dropped to the sidewalk, darted across the
road and leaped at the wall of Markham's Mill. He managed to
get his hands on the top of the wall. He pulled himself up, and
the last things he saw as he scrambled over were the backs of the
two plain-clothes men. They had not seen him.

In the quiet mill yard he circled a heap of scrap metal which looked like the broken frames of old looms, and went in search of the boilerhouse. He walked round a heap of engine coal, and found the boilerhouse door. As he hoped, it was a plain, heavy door with a big, old-fashioned lock. He went to work on it with his piece of wire. It took him ten minutes to get into the place, and two minutes to relock the door when he was inside.

13.

P.C. Larry Vincent had served for six years in the Granchester force, most of the time as an ordinary "bobby" in uniform. His only experience in detective work had been gained during a three-months training spell in the C.I.D., and by watching and listening intelligently when his duty had taken him to the scenes of major crimes. He had learned only the rudiments of the gentle art of keeping observations upon the person, better known as tailing or shadowing.

Nevertheless, when he followed Rosa Vizard into the bar lounge of the Devonshire Arms, his manner was right. He walked with the air of an unconcerned but confident stranger, at a leisurely pace which gave him time to look around. And his eyes were good. He saw things thoroughly while barely seeming to glance at them.

At first, in the small lobby which he entered, there was nothing much to see except two doors marked "Ladies" and "Gentlemen," and the double-leaf frosted-glass door of the bar lounge itself. He went to the glass door and eased it open half an inch. The opening gave him a narrow view diagonally across the big room, to another door which was at the far corner. He could also see the end of the bar, which occupied one whole side of the room.

Rosa had walked right across the room, to a place within a few feet of the further door. She was sitting at a table, on a bench seat with her back to the wall. It was a position which enabled her to see most of the room and its occupants. At this time in the evening there were not many occupants. Later, Larry knew, the place would be packed.

He gently closed the door and turned away. He lit a cigarette, and thinking that it might be better if he did not seem to be treading on Rosa's heels, he waited there a little while.

When the cigarette was done he went outside and walked to the main entrance of the place. He passed through the main lobby and located the other door of the bar lounge. He entered, and without looking at anybody in the place, he dropped into the first seat inside the door. This was a bench seat like Rosa's and not six feet away from her. His hat was already in his hand, though that ornate, almost sumptuous room was a resort where male customers did not always remove their hats. He put the hat on the seat beside him, then he looked around, apparently for a waiter. His glance met Rosa's. She was eying him in cool appraisal. He looked away.

He surveyed the room. The bar was splendid, glittering with mirrors, polished glasses and colorful bottles under brilliant light. Even the beer pumps were decorative. The bench seat, comfortably upholstered in green moquette, ran round the remaining three sides of the room. The rest of the place was crowded with small oaken tables—Larry thought that there must be at least sixty—each with four small upholstered chairs. The walls were paneled in light oak to shoulder height, and above the panels were sporting scenes in modernistic style, done in plaster in bas-relief. The carpet was as rich and green as a meadow in spring. The three barmaids were attractive. The four white-coated waiters looked like competent bouncers. It was that certain something about the waiters which informed the stranger that the place was perhaps too good for its regular customers.

The thirty or forty people in the place made a sparse gathering. Larry looked them over, without seeming to do so. He was glad to see that he did not know any of them. He did not want a chance acquaintance to engage him in conversation.

A waiter came, and Larry ordered a glass of beer. The waiter went to the bar, paid for the beer, brought it, accepted payment and put the cash in his pocket.

Larry lit another cigarette. Then Rosa caught his glance again. She was looking at him, and holding a cigarette in a helpless way, as if she were too modest to ask for a light. It was a pose that would not have deceived a romantic lad of seventeen.

Willing to play along, Larry brought out his lighter. He stretched a long arm, and she leaned toward him with cigarette to lips. When she sat up straight with her cigarette going, she had moved two feet nearer to him.

"Thank you," she said.

"Not at all," he replied.

"I must get some matches," she went on with a little laugh of assumed embarrassment. "You see, I'm not used to being out alone."

"I'm not surprised," was the gallant rejoinder. "A girl as good-looking as you won't go short of company."

"That's the point. One likes a change of company. One gets tired of the same old faces."

"Do you often come in here?" he asked politely.

"No, very seldom."

"It reminds me of Blackpool. It's like a Blackpool pub."

For the first time she was natural. And she was eager. "Give me Blackpool every time," she said warmly. "It does me a power of good. I wish I lived there."

"There's plenty goes on in Blackpool," he admitted tactfully. "Are you going there this summer?"

She gave the matter serious consideration. There were, after all, many wonderful places she had never seen. "I don't know," she answered. "We—I might go further afield. France or Italy, happen."

128

"That'll cost plenty."

"Oh, I don't know," she said, with the air of one to whom the question of cost is not important. "I'd need a lot of new clothes," she added dreamily.

"It may not be too expensive if you go on your own. Not like taking a family."

"Are you married?" she asked.

"No," he said, and her smile approved of his bachelorhood.

"Are you?" he asked.

"Yes, but I don't live with my husband. We don't get on together."

"In that case it's usually best to part, unless there are children," he commented, wondering if there could possibly be a more trite dialogue anywhere than this. The business of mutual inquiry between newly met people was usually pretty dull, he reflected, because most people lived humdrum lives.

She ignored the remark about children. "What's your name?" she asked.

"Larry. What's yours?"

"Rosa."

"A nice name. It suits you."

"It's right enough," she said. "What do you do for a living?"

He was ready for that one. "I work in a lawyer's office."

She was impressed. "Are you going to be a solicitor?"

"I don't know. It depends. I'll at least be a managing clerk sometime."

"Does that pay much money?"

"Enough," he replied. "Our managing clerk doesn't seem to do so badly."

"You'll know a lot about the law, I expect."

"I know a little," he said modestly.

"If somebody dies without making a will, do the next of kin share the money equally?"

He knew very little about civil law, and he was not sure of the answer. He took a chance. "They usually do," he said. And to make it sound better: "If there is no question of property in entail."

"Entail? What's that?"

"Like these big estates, where some property has to stay in the family. The eldest son inherits it."

She was not interested in entail. "Suppose it's somebody who has no brothers or sisters, but his father and mother are still alive," she persisted. "Are they the next of kin?"

"Oh, yes."

"Thank you," she said, apparently satisfied.

"Do you live around here?" he asked.

"Along the road," she answered shortly, and it was obvious to him that she had no intention of telling him exactly where her home was.

He finished his beer. "Will you join me in a drink?"

She said that she would have a gin and bitter lemon, and without further encouragement she moved the remaining distance so that she was sitting by his side. When a waiter had brought the drinks and gone away, Larry said: "Plenty of excitement in Burnside this week-end, isn't there?"

"What do you mean?"

"The escaped convict. And the little girl missing. That's getting middling serious, you know."

"It's awful," she said vaguely.

"Do you know her at all?"

"Let's not talk about it," she said briskly. "It depresses me. Let's talk about nice things."

Nice things were, apparently, favorite drinks, favorite foods, holidays, films and film stars, radio and television personalities and the clothes they wore. It was clear that Rosa spent a lot of time thinking about clothes. Now she put her thoughts into words. Larry listened heroically.

"These actresses and their minks," she said when he was beginning to think that even she was talked out on the subject. "If I wanted to be that way, I could give a man a hell of a good time for a fur coat."

"Oh, you could, could you?" a new voice interrupted.

They looked up. The man whom Larry knew as John Kegan had entered the room, and standing unperceived beside the door he had overheard Rosa's last remark.

"Hello," she said, after a brief, stricken silence.

Kegan looked at her with a baffling expression. At that moment he seemed to be more amused and curious than angry. "I thought I might find you in this nanny hole," he said. "You always come here when you think you'd like a change, don't you?"

Rosa did not reply. Kegan inclined his head toward Larry. "Introduce me," he said.

"This is Jack Kegan, this is Larry," said Rosa lamely.

Neither man offered to shake hands, but Larry acknowledged the introduction by standing up. He wanted to be on his feet when the trouble started.

The movement was noticed. Two of the waiters drifted gently toward the group by the door. In their experience, when a man rose to his feet, it was not with the intention of being polite.

"Larry who?" Kegan demanded.

"I don't know," Rosa replied.

"Just Larry," said the owner of the name.

"Do you do your drinking here?"

Larry shrugged.

Kegan's manner hardened. "No talkee, eh? How long has this been going on, with my woman?"

"Nothing has been going on. We just met, for the first time."

"Oh. And do you think you're going to meet again?"

"I don't know. I haven't decided," said Larry, who saw no reason why he should bow the head to Kegan.

"Ah, one of the hard boys. If I was trying to like you, you'd be proper distressing me, you would."

"I couldn't care less about you and your likes," said Larry, suddenly finding that he had a strong antipathy for this man who was Dessie Kegan's father, squabbling in a pub anent the conduct of a woman who was not his wife, while the question of the child's fate became more and more serious.

Kegan measured Larry with his eyes. Rosa noticed the look, and understood it. Her poise and composure returning, she said with malice, "He's too big for you. And ten years younger."

That was when Kegan began to get really angry. He gave her a glance of hatred, and said: "He looks like a copper to me."

"Well, he isn't," she answered, but there was sudden doubt in the quick stare she turned in Larry's direction.

Larry observed the waiters. He sat down. One of the waiters drew nearer. "No trouble, I hope?" he said to Kegan with heavy politeness.

The question was ignored. Apparently the waiter did not like his questions to be ignored. "Are you going or staying?" he asked with an edge to his voice.

"I'm going," said Kegan. "I wouldn't drink in this dump if it was free."

"In that case, it might be a good idea if you got moving."

Kegan made no direct reply to the suggestion, but to Rosa he said: "Come on, you!"

For a moment she looked as if she might defy him, then she shrugged and picked up her handbag. As she stood up she said:

"Good night, Larry. See you sometime."

"Like hell you will," Kegan snapped, rage suddenly boiling up. "Go on, get out!"

She went out, and he followed her. The waiter said: "Once a gentleman, always a bloody toff. Don't you meet 'em?"

He went away. People who had been staring at the scene turned their attention elsewhere. Larry finished his drink and slipped out of the place.

He went through the main doorway cautiously. In the entrance he stood still, looking for Rosa and Kegan. They had crossed the forecourt and were turning toward home, walking a yard apart.

Kegan's head was turned toward the girl, as if he were speaking to her. He reached a peak of exasperated self-pity, and raised his voice. "You do this to me at a time like this!" he exclaimed in passionate reproach. "What sort of a woman are you? Have you no feelings at all?"

Apparently she said something in reply, because he shouted: "I won't shut up! I'll tell the world you're no good! No damn good at all! And if you speak to me like that again, I'll flatten you!"

Perhaps she did not speak again, because he made no attempt to strike her. They went along Wales Road, and from his attitude it seemed that he still had much to say to her. But he did not raise his voice again.

Larry went across the forecourt in a direction slanting away from the people he followed. He crossed the road, and sauntered along close to some shops which were there. He remained a good distance behind the other two, being conscious of the possibility that Kegan might turn and look for him.

The pair trailed unhappily on their way until they drew level with the Flying Dutchman. There, Rosa stopped and turned. Kegan walked on a pace or two, then stopped and faced her. Larry did not stop. He drew nearer. Something in Rosa's attitude, even at that distance, told him that she would be silent no longer. She was going to say what was in her mind.

She said it with the full power of her voice. "So I've done this and I've done that, but what the hell have you ever done? When I took you into my home you were going to do everything. You were going to be a traveler and make big commissions, and we were going to have a car. Everything was going to be lovely. Traveler, ha ha! Selling brushes with one foot in the door. You couldn't sell ice cream in Timbuktu. You and your big ideas! What the hell have you ever done for *me*? I'm the mother of your child too, don't forget."

She paused for breath. He said nothing in remonstrance. She started again. "Oh, sure you've done your best. You've done your best all right. A bare living and a bastard to nurse, that's what you've given me. You haven't put a thing into my house except a yelling brat. Never a coat for my back and never a holiday have you given me. I haven't had a new thing since I stopped working. *That's* what you've done for me."

He stretched out a hand to her, but not aggressively. She knocked the hand aside. "Don't you touch me!" she shrilled. "You've had your say, and I'm having mine. When this job is all settled you'll do right by me, or else I'll find a man who can give me what I want. Now I'm going for a drink and you can go to hell."

She turned and ran from him, across the road and through the doorway of the Flying Dutchman. For a little while Kegan remained where he was, then he slouched despondently after her.

Larry took up a position from which he had the door of the inn in view. He reflected glumly that the rest of the evening's work would be very dull. Probably Kegan and Rosa would stay in the Flying Dutchman until closing time, and then, amicably or otherwise, they would make their way home.

The tie between them appeared to be stronger than Larry had thought. That evening it had stood a lot of strain, but Rosa had been in no doubt that it would stand more. And she had been right. After she had spoken her mind and made her threat, Kegan had meekly followed her. The bond between those two people was still not seriously damaged. Not yet.

But what had he, P.C. 942 Vincent, got to report? There had been a quarrel, recriminations, a threat to break up the happy home: a common argy-bargy between a common man and a common woman. Contact had been made with the subject of observation, and all she had talked about had been the law of inheritance, clothes and—what else?—holidays. The inheritance business undoubtedly had something to do with Dessie Kegan. It was something to report, though on the face of it no more than a natural interest in possible benefits was shown. And as for the other things, well, the woman was just crazy for clothes.

"So what?" Larry Vincent wanted to know. "Lots of women are crazy for clothes, and there are folks who get themselves into debt for the sake of a few days' holiday at Blackpool."

14.

WHEN he had entered the boilerhouse of Markham's Mill, Guy Rainer found an unlocked door which led him to the engine room. This was a long room with tall windows, so that he stood in gloom only a little deeper than the starlit, lamplit darkness out of doors. The floor of the room was nothing more than a railed gallery which ran around the horizontal engine. The shiny metal parts of the engine glistened faintly.

Guy doubted if anyone outside would be able to discern movement in there, but he kept his head down when he passed the row of windows. When he straightened at the further end of the gallery he brushed against something. At first he was startled, and then he discovered that he had touched one of several garments which hung against the wall on a row of hooks. One of the garments was a denim jacket, and in a side pocket he found a box of matches and a packet of Woodbines. There were five cigarettes in the packet. Guy would not have been more pleased if he had found a five-pound note.

A door near the row of hooks allowed him to move forward into a place of absolute darkness. His groping left hand found another door, an outer door, he guessed. His right hand touched a wooden handrail. He reached along the rail, and let it guide him down a flight of ten wooden stairs. At the foot of the stairs he felt the coldness of a stone floor. He sat down and put on his boots.

There was still no glimmer of light to be seen, so he reasoned that he could safely make some illumination of his own. He struck a match and saw that he was in a big basement room. He also saw that there was no inflammable material anywhere near him. He sat down on the stairs again and lit a Woodbine. He inhaled luxuriously. The cigarette was almost as enjoyable as he had imagined it would be. Temporarily, it lifted fatigue from him and killed his hunger.

He carefully extinguished the butt of the cigarette, and stood up. He struck another match, and moved along in its light. The room contained waste bags, some half filled, some ready for sending away. Near one wall there was a bench where shuttles were neatly piled, and skeps containing old picking sticks, pickers and leather thongs which, he supposed, had been taken from the obsolete looms which were broken up in the yard. He struck another match and moved across the room. He saw the mill's "hoist," which was a big, open lift used for moving warps and other heavy objects from floor to floor. The hoist was at the basement floor, and Guy was wondering if he would use it when he espied another flight of stairs in the corner.

He went up the stairs. There was a turn halfway up, but no door at the top. There, he found that he was in the big main warehouse of the mill. Many windows threw light upon the sloping inspection tables which occupied two sides of the room. There was a row of machines whose purpose he could not guess, but most of the floor space was taken up by orderly piles of cotton cloth in bolts or "pieces."

The piles of cloth were eerily white. The place was still. Guy would have been glad of the company of a friendly cat. Loneliness was beginning to affect him.

He found an inner door. It was a swing door, of wood with a metal covering. When he pushed it open, it creaked loudly enough to frighten him. He stood holding the door, looking into a great shed. Faint light came down through long rows of overhead windows, showing him the equally long rows of the looms which had woven the cloth he had seen. The looms were clad in white cloth and gray warp. Above them shone the silver-steel driving shafts and the big pulleys with their slanting pattern of driving belts. He imagined what noise there would be when the shafts were turning and all the looms were running. He had heard that deafening clatter many a time, because he had occasionally worked as an electrician in factories before he had gone to work on ships. Now, the silence oppressed him. The place was quieter than the graveyard where he had so recently been concealed.

He closed the door of the shed and returned to the warehouse. He assumed that if the weaving shed was at one side, the offices would be at the other, near to the main door. In the office there might be money, of which he was, or would be, in need. He made his way between piles of cloth worth many thousands of pounds, and went in search of the petty cash. He found a door, a very solid door of polished wood. His groping fingers found a keyhole, but no handle. He struck another match, shielding the light with his body. He shook his head and sighed when he saw that the door was secured by a modern mortise lock.

He worked at the lock with his piece of wire, but gave up when his strong hands began to tremble with fatigue. He guessed that this was only the door leading to the entrance lobby or passage. Beyond it, in the lobby, there would be another locked door barring the way to the office.

He went down into the basement and had a smoke while he considered the situation. First, a good hiding place would have to be found, in case the daylight brought a search party. A half-filled waste bag was a good hiding place, but not good enough. There was the hoist. It would be very low-geared, like all open lifts. He wondered if it would move slowly enough for a man riding down from ground floor to basement to jump out and fling himself into the bottom of the shaft, so that he was concealed by the hoist itself when it settled into position. No policeman would ever dream that a man could operate a hoist and also conceal himself in the bottom of the shaft.

He went to look at the hoist. To his surprise, he found that it

137

had a modern push-button board instead of the old-fashioned pull ropes usually seen in mill hoists. He stepped into the hoist and pressed the "G" button, in the hope that the thing had not been switched off at the main. The hoist began to rise slowly, just as slowly as if it were carrying a ton of machinery. Guy counted. He had counted off eleven seconds before the hoist shuddered gently to a stop. Eleven seconds! What the hell, he thought, a man could run a hundred yards in eleven seconds. The thing was easy.

He took four matches from the box and held them in a little bundle in his fingers. He held the matchbox ready in the other hand. He pressed the "B" button, and the hoist began its slow descent. He went down on his knees, struck the four matches, and vaulted out of the hoist by their flaring light. He landed on his feet, and stood looking into the bottom of the shaft. Dimly seen, the well of the shaft was four feet deep, with the usual years-old scattering of rubbish in the bottom. He estimated that he had ample time to get into the well before the hoist settled into place.

Then he perceived the great fault in his scheme. Hidden in the bottom of the shaft, he would be trapped there until the hoist came into use on Monday morning. That would be better than being caught by the police, but not much better. He decided that the hoist shaft must only be used if he could not find some other hiding place.

He went up to the warehouse again, and continued his exploration. He worked round to the farthest end of the inspection tables, and found a tiny glassed-in subsidiary office. There would be no money here, he decided. This was the place from which the warehouse foreman supervised his staff. He found the doorless entrance and looked in. On the small, high desk, silhouetted dimly, he discerned a telephone. He stepped forward and peered to examine it. It was not an internal-line thing, but a genuine telephone, a means of communication with the outside world.

The last group of Saturday night's customers straggled out of the Dog and Duck Inn at five minutes to eleven, and the doors were closed behind them. When the cheerful, chattering group had dispersed, Martineau and Cassidy left the dark doorway which was their observation point, and approached the inn. They paused beside the window of the saloon bar, which was, incidentally, the only bar of the little place. The lower half of the window was of fancy opaque glass, the upper half was transparent.

Martineau looked up and down the street. "Give me a leg up," he whispered.

He steadied himself with his hands on the wall near the side of the window while the powerful Irishman stooped, put both arms round his legs, and lifted him. He peeped into the bar, and saw four people. An elderly man, an elderly woman, a young barmaid and a middle-aged waiter were busy, washing up, cashing up, sweeping up. Martineau waited a little while and peeped again. There was no young man who answered to the description of David Barber.

"Right," he whispered, and Cassidy put him down. "David doesn't seem to be home yet," he said as they returned to their doorway.

At ten minutes past eleven the waiter and the barmaid left the premises together, by the front door. They walked away. The door was closed again, and bolts were noisily shot into place. The lights in the bar were turned off.

The night grew quieter. There was no motor traffic in Jasmine Street, and there were very few pedestrians. The peace was disturbed once by a gang of raucously hilarious youths, who did not perceive the two big, motionless men in the doorway.

Martineau thought about his lost week-end; a week-end half over, and still no trace of either Dessie Kegan or Guy Rainer. A day and a night spent in futile search and fruitless inquiry. The policeman's lot. He had gone to see Clay before leaving Headquarters, and had found him recovering from a hard session in the Interrogation Room with Albert Vizard.

"I got nowhere with him," the stout superintendent had growled. "I got the feeling he knew something I didn't know, and I kept going at him till he went ga-ga on me. I had to call the doctor. The doc gave me a black look and wrapped him up for the night. Says he has to be left alone. That's nice, isn't it? A prime suspect and he has to be left alone!"

Martineau had sympathized, and then Clay had told him about an incident in Burnside that evening. A young man had tried to rob a petrol station in Derbyshire Road, with a dummy gun. He had been chased by a garage hand and a policeman. The policeman, not being near enough to see the man he pursued, had assumed that he was Guy Rainer. The young man had been seen in St. Mary's churchyard and caught in the grounds of Holly Lodge, but the rumor that he was Rainer had caused a temporary relaxation of vigilance throughout the division.

Martineau had left Headquarters then, thinking about the false alarms which so often raise the hopes of the P.C. on patrol: the "big jobs" which turn out to be nothing. The capture of the lad with the dummy pistol had been a good enough case for an ordinary Saturday night, but the revelation of his identity had nevertheless been anticlimax. In the collective mind of the Granchester force that night there were only two important matters, the Kegan job and the Rainer job.

So Martineau waited, and at five minutes to twelve he saw a young man walking along the street. This one was tall and lightly built, wearing a light gray suit and no hat. His hair shone like silver gilt as he passed under a street light. He looked neither to right nor left as he made his way to the rear of the Dog and Duck. A door was slammed.

The young man was followed by his weary "tail." Martineau stopped the follower, questioned him briefly, and sent him home.

A minute later, Detective Constable Ducklin appeared furtively at the corner near the inn. He and a colleague named Evans had been detailed to watch the rear of the building. He crossed the road and joined Martineau and Cassidy.

"A young fellow who might be David Barber has just gone in by the back door," he reported. Martineau murmured "Good," and told the man to stay with Cassidy. Now was the time for something to happen. Rainer would know his friend's Saturday habits. If he had access to a telephone, his call would come during the first hour after midnight. So Martineau hoped. It was all too probable that Rainer would not make any call.

In the back yard of the inn, the chief inspector found Evans lurking in an open cart shed whose deepest shadows were dark enough to hide any watcher. Opposite the shed, light showed through the curtains of the kitchen window.

"Not bad cover, this," he commented in a low voice.

"Very handy, sir," said Evans. "We heard the phone ringing quite plainly from here. I listened at the window, but I couldn't hear what was being said."

They waited in silence for about ten minutes, then a light appeared in a bedroom overlooking the yard. They saw the elderly woman draw the curtains. The light in the kitchen did not go out.

They waited. The light upstairs went out.

At twelve-twenty-five the telephone rang. Immediately, before anyone upstairs could have time to get out of bed and look down into the yard, Martineau went a-tiptoe to the kitchen window. He removed his hat and very gently put his ear to the glass. Intermittently he heard a man's voice, but he could not distinguish any words. Once or twice the voice rose sharply, as if in protest.

"Whatever it is," Martineau decided, "he doesn't want to do it."

He did not hear the sound as the receiver was put down, and he was startled when the kitchen light suddenly went out. He made a silent leap to the side of the window, and stood close to the wall. He noticed that Evans had retreated into the deepest shadow of the shed.

Flat against the wall, the inspector could not see the window, but he did hear the slight movement of the curtain runner as the curtains were parted and then pulled close.

Then Evans emerged from the shed and beckoned urgently. Martineau joined him and they went out of the yard. "He peeped out," said Evans. "I got the impression he was coming out."

They crossed to the corner of a back street. Evans crouched at the corner and watched from a little over knee height. Martineau stood behind him.

They heard the back door of the inn close quietly, then the tall figure of David Barber emerged from the yard. He went to the front of the building and turned the corner, walking along Jasmine Street in the direction of Wales Road. His extraordinarily blond hair made him clearly identifiable when he passed under a street light.

"You stay here and watch the pub," Martineau said to Evans. "We don't know exactly what the move is yet."

He went to Jasmine Street. The subject of observations was sixty yards away. The chief inspector flitted like an oversize specter across the street, and joined the two men in the doorway. "There he goes," he remarked unnecessarily. "Now you know the drill. You stay here, Ducklin. I'll do the tailing. Cassidy contacts the car and then follows me."

"Yessir," the men said.

With that, Martineau went after Barber. He was careful, keeping at a good distance and showing himself as little as possible. Twice he saw Barber stop and pretend to look in a shop window, but each time he was able to get out of sight before he could be discerned. He looked back once himself, and was just able to see Cassidy. That was right. Cassidy had to be in a position to receive signals.

When Barber began to walk southward along Wales Road, Martineau guessed where he was going. He stopped and beckoned to Cassidy, and sent a message through him to the following car. From the car a message was relayed to Devery's car which was in the vicinity of Carmarthen Street, to warn the sergeant of the approach of the fair-haired young man.

Barber did go to Carmarthen Street. When he arrived, there

was no police officer in sight. Every one of the small houses on the street was in darkness. One solitary street lamp burned halfway along the row. Barber went without hesitation to the house which was nearest to the light. He may have taken that as a guide, or he may have known the house well. He stood and looked up at a bedroom window.

Watching from the nearest corner, Martineau saw Barber take something from his coat pocket and throw it at the window. It was a handful of small objects which twinkled in the light. They struck the window and tinkled as they landed on the ground. Martineau guessed that they were metal caps from beer bottles.

Barber threw a second handful of caps, and then a light appeared in the bedroom. A sash window was pushed open. A man's face appeared.

"What the hell . . . ? Hello, Dave! What the devil do you want at this time of night?"

"Let me in, Alan. I've got to see you. It's important."

"Is this some sort of a gag?"

"No, Alan. I'm dead serious."

"Righto. I'll be down in a minute."

The window was pulled down. Barber went and stood with his back to the door, waiting for it to be opened. Martineau withdrew the half a head he had been showing, because that was the time for the blond man to take a good look up and down the street.

When Martineau looked again, Barber had lit a cigarette. It glowed brightly as he inhaled hungrily. Nerves, the watching policeman thought. Always the cigarette was craved in times of stress.

The door of the house opened and closed, and Barber was no longer on the doorstep. But no light appeared in the house, and Martineau guessed that the two men had gone into the kitchen at the back. He crossed over with the intention of going along the back street to the rear of the house. A man emerged from a doorway in the cross alley. It was Devery.

143

"I've been watching you, sir," he said.

"They've gone into the back kitchen," said Martineau. "I'm going to listen at the window."

"I doubt it, sir."

In the darkness the senior officer stared. "Why not?" he demanded.

"There's a wee doggie in a kennel in the back yard. He doesn't bark very loud, but loud enough. I found him when I was casing the joint. Luckily there was nobody in the house at the time."

"In that case we'd better keep our distance," said Martineau. "We'll just have to wait and see what happens."

They waited twenty minutes. During that time the light reappeared upstairs, and went out again. Then the two men emerged from the house. Clare, a somewhat shorter and sturdier man than Barber, was carrying a brown-paper parcel which was just small enough for him to hold comfortably under one arm. Clothes, Martineau thought. Clothes for one who needed them badly.

The two friends made for Wales Road, and for the corner where the watching policemen lurked. Their diagonal course across Carmarthen Street was an indication of the direction they would go along the main road. Martineau sent Devery running to clear the way, and himself ran to a further corner so that they could get ahead of him. Clare and Barber passed on without seeing him.

Devery had time to arrange matters in Wales Road. When the two men appeared, and turned in the direction of Holly Road, there were no policemen in sight except Devery, far ahead of them and going away, apparently a late wayfarer like themselves. Thus, as they went along, any policeman who happened to be in their path was forewarned in time to fade away along a side street, not to emerge until they had passed.

The two did not hurry, evidently assuming that undue haste would arouse suspicion in the mind of any member of the constabulary who saw them. They sauntered, consciously leisured and casual. Normally, at that time of night, any policeman they met would have had a question or two to ask about the brown-paper parcel, however innocent they looked. But perhaps they were not aware of that.

Uninterrupted and unalarmed, they reached the crossroads where Holly Road and Eden Street met at Wales Road. They went on, along that part of the road which ran between the blank walls of Holly Lodge and Markham's Mill, and they walked on the Markham's Mill side. Devery was no longer in sight ahead of them, and Martineau was invisible in their rear.

The situation was temporarily difficult for Martineau. He was compelled to allow his two "clients" to get further ahead of him than he liked. He dared not yet show himself under the bright lights of the crossing, nor dare he enter the bare stretch of road beyond it until the men he followed were a considerable distance further along the road. He crouched behind a pillar box, with just the top of his uncovered head showing above it. He watched from there, and hoped that Devery, wherever *he* was, would have the wit to realize what was happening.

The two men reached the further corner of the mill premises, and turned the corner to go along the side street there. And as they turned the corner both men looked back and saw an apparently deserted road. Martineau was able to see that movement, and he knew what it meant. The men were getting near to the scene of some action.

Eager now, he ran, moving as lightly as possible on his toes. He was panting when he reached the further corner of the mill. He stood listening for a moment, then he peeped round the corner. He saw Clare and Barber sixty or seventy yards along the side street, walking away from him. He waited until they passed a street light, and then he saw that Clare was no longer carrying the parcel. Obviously the parcel had been thrown over the wall into the mill yard. Therefore it seemed likely that Guy Rainer was hiding somewhere on the premises. Probably he had telephoned Barber from the mill itself.

Martineau expressed his relief in a sigh. At least one part of the week-end's double quest was nearly over. "If I don't get Rainer this time," he breathed, "I'll put my ticket in."

15.

IMMEDIATELY he understood that Guy Rainer was hiding in Markham's Mill, Martineau realized that there must be no noise. As he stood watching the retreating forms of Clare and Barber, he surmised that Rainer might be near to him at that very moment, listening on the other side of the wall. Or he might be crouched somewhere in hiding, watching the bundle as it lay in the yard, waiting a while to make sure that his friends had not unwittingly betrayed him. If a head appeared above the wall, looking for the bundle, the situation would be clarified for him. If he heard a sound of voices he would be running again, getting away from the mill before it could be surrounded. And, Martineau ruefully remembered, he certainly could run.

The inspector looked about him. Not a living soul could he see. He stepped to the curb and beckoned. Three men appeared from the shadows along the street which ran along the back of Holly Lodge to St. Mary's church. Ahead, along Wales Road, two indistinct figures appeared in the distance. At the crossroads Cassidy showed himself, and at intervals behind him were more men.

The men from St. Mary's Street were the first to arrive. As they drew near, Martineau raised a warning finger, and they halted. He put the finger to his lips, and they understood. He cocked his thumb in the direction of the mill, and they nodded. With two gestures he sent two of them to the two unwatched corners of the mill premises. The third man was the detective inspector of that division, a man who was probably more keen to lay hands on the escaped prisoner than Martineau himself was. This was the man who would rightfully have protested against Martineau's unsupervised activities in the division, had he not known that the C.I. from Headquarters was acting on the instructions of Clay, the supreme boss of the Granchester C.I.D. It was a bold D.D.I. who would willingly cross swords with Clay.

Martineau took the D.D.I. with him, across the road and into St. Mary Street so that they could talk. "Rainer's in the mill," he whispered. "There's been a parcel dumped over the wall two minutes ago. We'd better surround the place, then go in and take him in daylight."

"I daresay that would be best," the D.D.I. agreed. "He's a fast mover. He could slip away from us in the dark."

"You see to it, will you? And I'll be back at the crack of dawn with the manager and the keys."

"Very good, sir," said the D.D.I. readily. The arrangement ensured that he would be in at the kill, and might even be the man to arrest Rainer.

They returned to Wales Road. Devery and a plain-clothes man arrived. Cassidy came, with three more men behind him. The D.D.I. took charge of all except Devery, who went back along Wales Road with Martineau.

The two men went in search of Martineau's car, which they found waiting for orders well back from the scene of operations. "Carmarthen Street," said the chief inspector as he climbed into the back seat.

The driver said "Yessir," and in a very short time he slowed to take the corner which would bring him into the street.

"Don't go round the corner," said Martineau. "Wait here and come when I whistle."

The two detectives left the car and went into Carmarthen Street. They waited in the scant cover of a house doorway across the street from Clare's house. In a few minutes Clare and Barber came in sight at the other end of the row of houses, having made their way home by streets which ran parallel to Wales Road.

They strolled along, conversing in normal tones. No doubt they thought that for them the danger was over. Their task was done, and now they had the satisfaction of having gone to the help of a friend in need. But their attitude changed when Martineau and Devery crossed to intercept them. For a moment Barber seemed about to turn and run, then he must have thought better of it and decided to stay with his friend.

The four men met at Clare's door, under the light of the street lamp. Before he spoke, Martineau stooped and picked up a beer-bottle cap. He looked at it, then tossed it up in the air and caught it. Clare watched him impassively, Barber was obviously apprehensive.

"Good morning," said Martineau.

"Morning," came the reply.

Martineau introduced himself, and then he said: "Are you David Barber?"

"Yes," said Barber.

"And you're Alan Clare?"

"Yes," Clare replied.

Martineau made a taut mouth and whistled shrilly. The four men stood in silence until the car stopped at the curb beside them. Martineau opened a rear door. "Get in," he said.

"Why? What for?" Clare demanded.

"Somebody wants to talk to you at Headquarters."

"Who?"

"Myself."

"Oh." There was a brief silence. "What do you want to talk about?"

"About a matter concerning a young man called Guy Rainer."

"I'm afraid we can't help you."

"I don't want help, *I* want confirmation," said Martineau. "And while we're about it I may as well tell both of you that anything you may say will be taken down in writing and may be given in evidence. Now get in the car."

They sat in the rear of the car, and Devery sat between them. Martineau took the seat beside the driver, who did not need to be told where to go. At Headquarters, it was not thought necessary to take Barber and Clare to the Interrogation Room. Martineau had them taken to his own office.

"Now," he said, as he sat at his desk, with the two men standing before him and Devery standing beside the door, "I'll just tell you something about the law. Guy Rainer was sent to prison after being found guilty of the felony of manslaughter. Therefore his escape from prison before the expiration of his sentence is another felony. Anyone who aids, abets, counsels or procures the commission of a felony is punishable to the same extent as the felon."

"We never helped anybody to escape from prison," Clare protested.

"No? Well, I'll put it this way, and open the book for you if you like. It is a felony for a felon to *be at large* unlawfully in any part of the Queen's dominions. To aid or abet this felony is punishable to the same extent. Is *that* clear?"

Both men nodded. They were not hardened criminals, but men who were normally honest and law-abiding. In different ways, their faces reflected their profound dismay. Martineau felt rather sorry for them. Perhaps, he thought, he was frightening them unnecessarily. The phrases he had recited so glibly were some which he had learned as a police recruit twenty years ago, when they had seemed awful to him, too.

"I don't know if a lenient view can be taken of this," he went on in a milder tone. "I can promise nothing, but it is just possible that helpful behavior right now might stand in your favor later. Just to let you know that we're not merely guessing, I'll tell you that we heard Barber receive a phone call. We followed him to your house, Clare. From there, you and he and a parcel were followed to Markham's Mill, where you got rid of the parcel. Rainer is in the mill, isn't he?"

"We don't know that," said Barber.

"Then he didn't tell you where he was phoning from?"

"No," said Barber, and Clare said: "You ass!"

Barber turned on his friend. "So I made a slip," he said. "What does it matter? He knows, all right. He's got us. So now we've got your wife to think about. It won't be so nice for her."

Clare did not speak, and Barber continued: "I shouldn't have listened. I should have put the phone down and left it off the hook. He had no right to ask us to do what we did and I should have told him so. I got you into this and now I'm going to try and get you out of it. We can't help Guy now, anyway."

He turned to Martineau: "It's true. Guy phoned me, he didn't say where from. He wanted me to get clothes from Alan—they take the same size in nearly everything—and sling them with some money over the wall of Markham's Mill yard at a certain place. I went to see Alan, and persuaded him to help. I shouldn't have let him come with me. I should have made him go back to bed. But I'll admit I was scared, and I was glad of his company."

Martineau asked: "Did you have any more instructions from Rainer, besides the business of the parcel?"

"No."

"Did he tell you about his intentions in the near future?"

"No, and that's the truth. I asked him, and he said it'd be better if I didn't know. He said he'd write to me sometime if he got clear away."

"What was in the parcel?"

"A brown tweed sports coat, gray flannel trousers, gray socks and brown shoes. A cream-colored shirt with two collars, and a reddish-brown tie, and a fawn tweed cap."

"What else?"

"There was a razor and a bit of soap and some handkerchiefs. Some cigarettes. A flashlight he asked for. And four one-pound notes and some loose change in one of the pockets of the sports coat."

"Anything else?"

"No, that's the lot. I provided the money and the cigarettes. Alan only provided the clothes because I persuaded him."

"Oh, shut up!" Clare growled bitterly. "We're in this together. Stop trying to whitewash me."

Barber was silent. There was no more to say.

Having made his arrangements with David Barber, Guy Rainer considered how and when he would pick up the parcel of clothes and money which he so greatly needed, if and when it should arrive. He had designated a spot along the further wall of the mill yard, where David would be in comparative darkness as he threw the parcel over the wall, but where the lights of Wales Road would make it visible as it lay on the ground inside the yard.

With regard to the actual getting of the parcel, his thoughts did not run on the same lines that Martineau's did some little time later. He assumed that his friend would not get rid of the parcel until he had made sure that there was nobody about. Therefore that moment, when there was nobody about, would be the best time to run and pick it up. Having made up his mind about that, he departed from the warehouse foreman's office and made his way through the basement and the engine room to the boilerhouse. There, he set to work and reopened the outer door. He let himself out and left the door unlocked, and crept round to the other side of the mill. There he hid behind some empty weft boxes, and fixed an unwavering glance on that part of the yard where the expected parcel would alight.

He waited, as he thought, for hours. He saw no movement, and heard none except the sound of an occasional car passing along Wales Road. But he was not restless or fidgety. He was rather surprised at his own serenity, and he reflected that inevitably a hunted outlaw like himself must develop some of the qualities of the wild. Every hour of stolen freedom was giving him an increasing fitness to survive. Prison and the bitterness of his fate had hardened his nature: it had conditioned him mentally for an ordeal. The ordeal itself, instead of fraying his nerves, had somehow strengthened them. He could wait for the moment of action without fretting away his strength. He believed that now he had a little of the hungry patience of a hunting cat. He was no longer surprised at the cool audacity of a fox. He realized that it was possible to live a life of ceaseless vigilance without being forever in a state of tension, that he could be both watchful and placid like the little beasts of the field or the kings of the jungle. "I'm getting used to it," he told himself.

He waited, and at last he heard the click of heels. There were two men walking unhurriedly, one with less frequent and rather heavier footfalls than the other. A tall man and one less tall, he assumed, and neither of them policemen because the sound of their footsteps was not deadened by rubber. He wondered if these were his friends. He prayed that they would be his friends.

"Both of them have come," he thought. "Sticking together, as ever." Dear old pals, jolly old pals. One for all and all for one. David at least did not like this business, he knew that. But still both of them had come to his assistance.

The footsteps went on to the corner. They turned the corner. They halted briefly, and the parcel sailed over the wall and landed and rolled in the yard. They went on.

Guy sprang to his feet and ran lightly across the yard. He picked up the precious bundle and ran back to cover with it. He crouched there, panting a little. He could still hear the footsteps of his friends, but he could not hear Martineau going soft-footed on the other side of the wall. He never knew that Martineau was there. He was creeping back to the boilerhouse while Martineau was silently beckoning to lurking policemen. He was locking himself in the mill while the policemen were spreading out to surround him.

He took the parcel to the inspection table in the warehouse

and opened it. He took the flashlight and the soap and razor to the basement, where there was a cold water tap and a gritty, unused sink. He shaved, and then he took a chance on being caught unprepared and stripped off all his clothes. When he had had a complete wash he dried himself with clean cotton waste and combed his wet hair with his fingers, then he returned to the warehouse and dressed himself in his new clothes. He found the money in the pocket of the sports coat, and counted it with approval. He returned to the basement and put his discarded clothes and boots, and the paper and string of the parcel, into a half-filled waste bag. He covered the sooty things with cotton waste, and washed his hands. Then he sat down and had a smoke. He was ready to go but, he decided, because it was Sunday he would not move before ten o'clock in the morning. Respectably dressed as he was now, he thought that he could venture out in daylight at that time. He would first survey the land from the upper windows of the mill, then he would go out.

He went to the top of the basement steps and sat down there. He decided that he could afford to close his eyes until daylight. Tired though he was, he slept lightly. His short crowbar, which he had retained, was on the floor by his hand.

He never knew whether it was the daylight or a premonition of danger which awakened him. He did not yawn or stretch, but sprang immediately to his feet. He went to a place from which he could look through the warehouse windows without being seen. It was another fine morning, and would be sunny. But he never noticed that. He had eyes only for the uniformed policeman who stood inside the yard with his back to the wall, facing the mill. Not far from the policeman there was another one, and beyond him another. It looked as if there might be two dozen bobbies surrounding the mill.

Guy did not waste a moment. He ran down into the basement and entered the hoist. He pressed the "G" button, and the hoist began its slow ascent. The eleven seconds seemed like an age. As the hoist came to a stop he heard an alarming sound: footsteps and voices in the passage beyond the polished door.

He pressed the "B" button, and the hoist began to go down. He vaulted out of it, into the basement, by the light of his torch. He turned, stooping, to jump into the well of the shaft, but the eager beam of the torch jumped ahead of him. It revealed the bottom of the shaft far more clearly than the flare of matches had done. What he saw did not stop him from jumping into the shaft, because he was already in motion, but it made him scramble out again as the hoist came down, and a very near thing it was.

He pressed the "G" button, and as the hoist went up he jumped down into the shaft. The light of his torch shone upon the prone figure of a child, a little girl, who was asleep, unconscious or dead. Her brown hair was matted with blood, and her head lay in a dried pool of it. But she was not dead. Even Guy's unpracticed finger could find a pulse.

The fugitive did not have to ponder about what he would do. The child looked near to death, and would have to be taken to hospital immediately. He picked her up, and lifted her to the basement floor. In doing so he found that his little crowbar was a hindrance, because he no longer had a rule pocket in his clothes. He climbed out of the well, slipped the bar up his right sleeve, and took the child in his arms. He carried her up the steps to the warehouse.

In the warehouse, Martineau, Devery, the D.D.I. and the mill manager were standing near the hoist, evidently having some discussion about it. Cassidy was the first to see Guy, and he started toward him. He barred the way.

"Stand clear!" said Guy sharply. "This child needs air."

The little head was drooping. Its bloody state was obvious. Cassidy was fond of children. He stood aside, and so did his companion, but they followed closely as Guy walked through the short corridor, past the inquiry window and the office door, to the outer door. By the time he got outside, the other men who had been in the warehouse were also crowding on his heels.

There was a small crowd of policemen outside the door—constables and sergeants and an inspector, traffic men, detectives, and a motorcycle patrol in leggings, gauntlets and a black leathern helmet. Guy stopped in the midst of them. Still holding his burden he half-turned, and Martineau pushed round to face him.

"Here, take her. She's still alive," Guy said. "I was going to hide at the bottom of the hoist shaft and I found her lying there."

Martineau held out his arms and took the child. All the policemen present looked on with compassion. While they were doing so, Guy ducked, turned, dodged through a thicket of blue-clad legs, and ran clear like a halfback going around the blind side of the scrum. The suddenness and quickness of the movement took everybody by surprise, even Cassidy who had been standing with hands ready, practically breathing down the fugitive's neck. Guy had achieved the seemingly impossible exactly as a crafty halfback achieves it.

The gateway from the mill yard into Eden Street had been opened wide. Two constables in uniform guarded the opening. Both of them were strong, heavy men. As he sped toward them Guy let his little crowbar slip down his sleeve into his right hand. He held it down at his side as he ran.

One of the policemen in the gateway stayed at his post. The other advanced a few feet and set himself for the tackle. Guy ran straight at him, then swerved slightly to the left at the last moment. As he swerved he held the crowbar like a sword and thrust cruelly, with all his strength, at the policeman's face. In sheer self-preservation the man jerked his head back and missed his tackle. His recoil hindered the view and movements of his colleague, who had to make a long dive to get at Guy. Guy skipped aside, striking with the bar as he did so. The man missed the tackle, but caught the bar with one hand. Guy left it with him, and sped out into Eden Street.

There were no policemen in Eden Street. Guy ran toward Wales Road, with a pack of policemen in full cry behind him.

One or two of those policemen were good runners, but Guy outdistanced all of them. He ran as he had never run before, in sheer dread now, not of arrest and imprisonment, but of the wrath of the men who pursued him.

In Wales Road, beyond the crossing, were four police cars, all stationary and facing toward Markham's Mill. Beyond them was a police motorcycle, facing in the other direction. Police drivers, disturbed by the sudden tumult, were getting out of cars. They were all getting out on the curb side. Guy ran along the "blind" side of the line, and was past before they could reach him. He seized the motorcycle, and in one swift, complex movement he pushed it off its stand and stooped to slip it into gear. He squeezed the clutch lever on the handlebars, and twisted open the throttle as he ran with the machine. He eased in the clutch. The engine was warm, and it fired immediately. He leaped into the saddle and shot away when there were but three feet of Wales Road between himself and his nearest pursuer's outstretched hand.

Standing in the yard of Markham's Mill, Martineau heard the roar of the motorcycle and made a shrewd guess. It was incredible, but he could credit it. Presently he learned that his guess had been accurate. Guy Rainer had once more eluded him.

"Well," he remarked philosophically, because the finding of little Dessie Kegan, alive, had been a great relief to him, "he certainly left *me* holding the baby."

16.

THE police motorcycle which Guy Rainer
had taken was a powerful machine, a big vertical-twin Triumph
Thunderbird, and thunder it did as it raced along Wales Road
in the quiet of early Sunday. In very little time after its running
start, the machine was traveling at eighty miles an hour. By the
time the first police car had turned round in the road and set off
in pursuit, Guy was nearly half a mile away.

There was an easy bend in Wales Road on the way to the
center of Granchester, and when he was round this bend, out of
sight of the distant policemen, Guy slowed and turned the motorcycle along a side street. In doing this he had no other purpose
than evasion. Already, he supposed, police drivers all over the
town would have been alerted by radio. They would be looking
out for him on every main road.

As he rode along byways, at a reduced speed now, he considered to what extent the Thunderbird could be of use to him.
As it burbled faithfully along he was aware of a touch of affection for it. A man's feeling for a good motorcycle is usually less
impersonal than his feeling for a car. He *rides* it. It responds to
every movement of his body, and its surge of power is more
clearly felt by him. At a slight turn of the throttle it will leap forward like a spurred thoroughbred, and like a thoroughbred it
needs a capable rider. Good old bike, Guy thought. He did not
want to smash it up, particularly since in smashing the bike he
would probably smash himself. Besides, he remembered, the
police had some extremely quick Jaguars. The Thunderbird
could run away from nine out of ten cars on the road, but with
a big Jag on its tail it would be a gone goose.

Guy decided that his chances of escape, or of finding a new

hiding place, would be better if he had a car. And with that thought came the realization that he was traveling deviously in the direction of Sheila Grayson's home. He knew very well where Sheila lived. Too well he knew it. In that house he had killed a man.

He guessed that Sheila would not help him now. But her father would, without knowing it. Her father had a car, and it was in a wooden garage at the end of his back garden. Guy vowed that if he couldn't open that garage, he would eat the tool that he was going to do it with. What model did the old man have now? he wondered. He hoped that it was one with a good turn of speed.

As he drew nearer to Parkhulme, Guy looked for a place where he could hide the Thunderbird. He grinned when he thought about the man from whom he had taken it. That speed cop would be having six sorts of fits, wondering if the reckless fugitive would smash his precious machine. Well, he would have to suffer a while longer. Guy did not want the motorcycle to be discovered for at least twenty-four hours.

He found a good hiding place for the motorcycle. It was an open yard which contained a number of lock-up garages. He wheeled the machine behind the furthermost garage, and opened the tool kit. He pocketed a screwdriver and, because he was now without a weapon, the heaviest spanner. He examined the garages, and found that they all had metal doors with locks which he could not turn. There was no point in wasting any more time. Old Man Grayson's car would have to be taken.

Saturday night was a restless night for Sheila Grayson. Her head ached, she was too warm in bed, she could not lie still. She could not stop worrying about poor little Dessie Kegan, and about poor headstrong Guy Rainer. She slept a little toward dawn, but she was awakened by the crack of daylight between the curtains of her bedroom. She got up and put on a dressing gown. She drew back the curtains and looked out at the morning. It was a grand morning. Her father's back garden was green and dewy, and there were birds on the lawn. She watched them a while, then put on slippers and went downstairs to make tea. She took the tray of tea things, and some aspirins, back to her room. She sat by the window drinking the tea, feeling no desire to go back to bed. She had a second cup and—something she did not more than once or twice a day—she smoked a cigarette.

Then she saw Guy Rainer walking along the unmetaled back road which ran behind the house. He was looking up at bedroom windows, and she drew aside to avoid being seen. She moved further back into the room, so that she could look out and still remain invisible to someone as far away as the end of the garden. She saw Guy open the back gate and walk round to the front of the garage, which was at the end of a straight drive which ran along by the wide of the house to the front gate. He looked all round, then he stooped to examine the lock of the big, double-leaf garage door. He took something from his pocket and moved to the side of the door. He began to do something to the topmost of the three hinges on that side. He had to work at eye level, and she could see his shoulders straining.

Sheila knew perfectly well what she ought to do. She had only to run downstairs to the telephone and dial 999, and the police would arrive in two or three minutes to take Guy away. That would be the best thing for him, she knew. Then he could finish his sentence and become a really free man. Nobody would bother him after that, because he wasn't a thief or a hooligan. Those were her thoughts while she watched Guy trying to break into her father's garage. She knew that he ought to be arrested and taken back to prison, but she could not bring herself to call the police. Nor would she rouse her father or Patricia and let one of them make the call, because that also would be a betrayal of Guy. She did not know whether or not her decision was affected by something akin to love, because now he seemed to be different somehow, but she just could not be the person by whose action he was caught and taken back to prison. Perhaps, she thought, the best thing she could do would be to let him see her. That would alarm him, and he would go away.

She went and stood at the window, but now he was engrossed in his work, and he did not look round. She opened the window wider, and pushed the curtain right back out of the way.

He heard the rattle of the curtain runner, and turned quickly. When he saw her he scowled, then his face cleared a little and he put a finger to his lips. He crossed the lawn and stood beneath the window. "Go back to bed," he said in a loud whisper.

She shook her head. "What are you doing to our garage?" she wanted to know.

He realized that she could hardly be expected to stand and watch while he stole her father's car. Unless he could get her out of the house and within his reach. Under his hand, so to speak.

He beckoned. "Come on out if you want to talk," he said. "And bring me something to eat, I'm starving."

He turned his back on her and went to the garage. She stood looking down at him, and remembering that yesterday he had hit her with an iron bar. But she also remembered that the deed had been done while she was willfully hindering him. She had assumed that he wanted to run after Patricia, and of course he had only wanted to run away. He had acted from instinct, when he was frantic with fear. She could not blame him, really.

She saw that it was her duty to persuade him to give himself up. She realized that once again she might fail to influence him, but at least she could try.

He looked round at her as she turned from the window. He saw her go, and he began to count the seconds. "I'm a fool," he decided. "Why didn't I go round to the front and cut the phone wires?"

In the house, Sheila wondered about Patricia. The two girls slept in two small, adjacent rooms which had been made out of one big one. The partition between the rooms looked solid, but it was actually quite flimsy. It was not by any means soundproof. Sheila went to the connecting door and opened it quietly. She looked in at Patricia. The curtains were drawn and she could not see her sister's face clearly, but she seemed to be asleep. She closed the door and went downstairs.

Guy was relieved when in no more than a minute's time he heard the sound of a closing door. Sheila was there, carrying a tray upon which there was a glass of milk and a big wedge of homemade fruitcake. It was obvious to him that she had not had time to stop on the way and dial 999. He wondered if she could have done that before she showed herself at the window. He would soon know about that, he reflected grimly. If the 999 call had gone in, the police would be arriving at any moment, with bells on. At the same time he thought it unlikely that the call had been made. If Sheila had called the police she would thereafter have kept out of his reach.

He put his screwdriver in his pocket, and reached for the cake and the milk. The cake was eaten in practically no time at all, and the milk followed it in one swig.

"Thanks," he said, wiping his mouth with the back of his hand, a habit he had acquired in prison. "Sorry about yesterday. I didn't intend to hurt either you or Pat. Are you all right?"

"Yes, I'm all right," she said. "But I still think you should give yourself up."

"No fear," he said. "I have a better chance now than ever I had. I've got some decent clothes. I found your missing kiddie, by the way."

"You did? Is she . . ."

"She's alive, but badly injured," he said. He told her about the finding of Dessie.

"And you escaped from all those bobbies?" she asked, in some awe.

"I did. I was dead lucky. I think it's fate. I'm fated to escape. Provided I stay on my toes."

She was immensely relieved about Dessie, but she wished she knew more about the child's condition. She decided that she would phone the police later in the morning. It would seem natural enough for her to ask for news.

Guy had resumed work with the screwdriver. She stood at his shoulder and noticed for the first time that the hinges of the garage door were on the outside, a silly arrangement from the point of view of security. Apparently Guy had noticed it at some time in the past, and he had remembered. He was removing the screws from the hinges. She saw that he need only free the hinges at one side, then he could get at the interior top-and-bottom bolts and open wide the entire double-leaf door as if it were in one piece.

He had to remove twelve screws in all. She saw him take out the third and throw it aside. He began to work on the fourth screw. It was rusted in, and the head was corroded. His screwdriver kept slipping out of the notch. He pushed and strained, and moved the screw a little. "I wish I had some penetrating oil," he muttered.

"Is it your intention to steal the car?" she asked.

"Borrow it," he corrected. "Your Dad will get it back undamaged."

He did not see the momentary look of surprise on her face. She was silent for a little while, then she said with some amusement: "Dad sold his car a year ago. He couldn't afford to run it after he retired."

He turned and stared at her. "You're kidding," he said.

"I'm telling you the exact truth."

"I ought to have looked," he muttered. He went to the small side window of the garage and rubbed sooty dirt from the glass. He shaded his eyes to peer at the dusky interior. At first he thought there was no car, and then he discerned something. He saw that it was a small, open two-seater.

"Whose car is that, then?" he growled as he returned to Sheila.

"It's Pat's. She'll be terribly cross if you take it."

"Pooh," he said, and resumed work on the hinges.

"Where could you go in it if you got it? You couldn't get out of Granchester."

"I could try," he said, and the rough outline of a plan came to him as he spoke. He would use the car to make his way to the far northeast side of the city. There he would leave it somewhere near a main road, to give the police the impression that he had got out of the city on that side, or that he was trying to travel in that direction. Then he would board a bus and ride back to the center of town. He thought that he would be safe enough on a bus which was inward bound. He would travel by bus to Burnside, and hide in the school until dark. After his first escape from Burnside, the police would never expect him to return, and there would be no guard on the school. Then after dark he would make his way to the big transport café off the Chester Road. He would hide somewhere near there until the right sort of vehicle pulled in. It would have to be a heavy lorry with a high, covered load of more or less irregular shape. Somehow he would wriggle in under the tarpaulin, and in the darkness he would ride out of the city that way.

"You're a fool," said Sheila. "They're bound to get you in time. If they don't, you'll be looking over your shoulder for as long as you live."

"They'll have to catch me before I go back to jail," he answered firmly. "Now you just keep quiet and let me get something done."

"I'll do no such thing."

"You will."

"I'm not going to stand here and watch you steal Pat's car. I'm going back indoors."

She was turning away. He put a detaining hand on her arm. He said: "You'd have been fain to stay with me at one time."

So he had known all along! Her pride was outraged. "Times have changed," she said.

He mocked her. "You don't like me now I'm only a poor jailbird trying to fly."

"Let me go!"

"Quiet!" he growled through set teeth. His hand moved from his pocket, and she saw that he was holding a spanner. She looked up into his face, and in his eyes she saw the blaze of fear and ferocity which a threat to his illegal liberty could produce. Pride could not sustain her. She cowered.

"Not a squeak will I have out of you," he whispered fiercely. "Make one little noise, and I'll hit you ten times as hard as I did yesterday. Now you stay here and be good."

After he had made his dry remark about holding the baby, Martineau handed little Dessie Kegan over to a detective named Murray, one of the few who had not gone chasing after Guy Rainer. "I'll get you a car," he said. "It'll be quicker than waiting for an ambulance."

"There's my car," said the mill manager.

"Thanks. We might need all ours. But will you lock the mill up first? I shall want to look around later in the morning, and I don't want anything to be disturbed. I'll leave a couple of men in the yard, just to make sure."

The manager locked the outer door of the mill. He led the way to his car. A sergeant in uniform got into the front seat with him, and Murray with the child took the rear seat.

"You two stay with her," said Martineau. "I want to be knowing every word she utters."

He watched the car move sedately away to hospital, and then Devery returned to report that Rainer had escaped on a police motorcycle.

"Quite a lad, isn't he?" the chief inspector said with a grin. "I vowed I'd put my ticket in if I let him slip me again, but I think I'll give myself another chance. Which way did he go?"

"Straight on Wales Road, toward town."

"H'm. He shouldn't get far, should he? Let us go and see what sort of transport we've got left."

164

They went to Wales Road. Only two C.I.D. cars were there. Fortunately they were radio cars.

"Get listening," said Martineau. "We want to know which way he's heading."

Devery went and sat in one of the cars. Martineau paced about nearby, meditatively smoking a cigarette. He thought about Guy Rainer. The fact that Rainer had produced Dessie Kegan had seemed at first to be a good reason for suspecting that he was the man who had kidnaped and injured her. But an examination of the circumstances provided no support for that suspicion. Rainer had practically given himself up to save the child. His subsequent dash for freedom had been a successful hundred-to-one chance. He could hardly have been able to send the letter which drew Sheila Grayson away from her usual homeward route on Friday, and it was even less likely that he could have known the details about Agnes Brown which made up the text of the letter. Nor was it easy to believe that he could have waited about near Markham's Mill to intercept Dessie. Probably he did not even know her. He had had neither motive nor opportunity to commit the crime.

Martineau wondered what Rainer's next move would be. Where would he go? It was almost a certainty that he would not go to the home of either of his two old friends. Had he any more trusty friends who would shelter him? Would a woman harbor him? Had he been sufficiently intimate with any woman at the time of his arrest, or before that? It was hardly likely. He had been head over heels in love with Patricia Grayson. Therefore *cherchez la femme* was not on the program, except in the doubtful case of Sheila Grayson. Would Rainer go to her as a last resort? And would she help him?

The big policeman made guesses about Miss Grayson's feelings toward Rainer. Yesterday Rainer had stroked her with an iron bar, but, before that incident, she had refused to give any information about his friends. She alleged that she had tried to persuade him to give himself up, but at no time had she made any attempt to betray him to the police. Women were queer folk, Martineau thought. Sheila Grayson might still have a soft spot for Rainer even after he had knocked her silly with his crowbar. She might be willing to help him, with or without persuasion.

Devery called from the car: "He turned off Wales Road somewhere, before he got to Chester Road. A car was waiting for him at Chester Road."

Martineau nodded. He continued to pace about. A group of his men—Cassidy, Cook, Ducklin, Evans—watched him from their listening post in the other car.

Five minutes later Devery reported: "Somebody in C Division has rung in. He heard a motorbike in one of the streets behind Hallam Road, not far from the Odeon. He didn't get a sight of it, but he thought it was traveling east."

Again Martineau nodded. Rainer might not be heading for Parkhulme, but he was certainly going in that direction. In any case, his direction was Martineau's direction. The chief inspector made up his mind.

"All right, Sergeant, we'll make a move," he said. "I'll go with Cassidy and Cook, in the other car. You'll follow in this one, with Ducklin and Evans. If we happen to get as far as Avon Road, you take the back of the house and I'll take the front."

"Right you are, sir," said Devery briskly. "If he's there, we won't miss him."

On the way to Parkhulme, a journey along empty roads, the crews of both cars remained in communication with Headquarters. For some time there was no further news of Rainer's movements. No man on a motorcycle had been seen or heard since the report from Hallam Road. All that the police could be reasonably sure of was that the fugitive was still held in the cordon of men and cars which kept the boundaries of the city.

In Martineau's mind there was a picture of Avon Road quiet and still in the early morning. As he drew nearer he wondered what he would do if he found nobody and nothing stirring when he arrived. He and his men would look around, and then they would have to get into hiding and wait in the hope that Rainer would come. That was not a pleasing prospect for tired and frustrated men.

Then, when there was less than half a mile to go, the great news came. There had been a 999 call. From Grayson, 49 Avon Road. At the time of calling Rainer was there, outside the house.

In the rear seat of Martineau's car, Cassidy gave a small cheer and told Cook to put his whip to the ass. In the other car there was excitement too. It drew alongside and Martineau waved for it to go on ahead, because its occupants had a little further to go.

Devery drove as fast as his car would go. He shot across Avon Road while Martineau was still some distance from it. He drove along the back road as fast as he could go and count the houses. He fixed the position of No. 49, and a moment later he heard Ducklin hiss: "There, by the garage!"

Devery saw Sheila Grayson standing there. She stared at the car, but she neither moved nor spoke. Beside her was a man, who had his back turned to the newcomers. He seemed to be doing something to the garage door. The sergeant stopped the car, and still Sheila made no attempt to warn her companion.

But as the policemen were getting out of the car the man heard something. He turned a startled face. When he saw Devery, he did not hesitate. He snarled an epithet and struck the girl across the face with the back of his hand. But even as he did that he was on the move. He ran down the drive to the front gate of the house, and the three detectives pounded after him.

Martineau was getting out of his car in front of No. 49 when he heard a shout and a rush of running feet. A fraction of a second later, Guy Rainer appeared. He vaulted the four-foot-high front gate, and ran across the wide suburban road with the nearest policeman six or seven yards behind him.

Guy ran straight at the site of the half-built filling station. The original roadside wall, a brick wall three feet high had not yet been demolished. Guy took the wall like a hurdler, clearing it easily. But he seemed to make a bad landing, because he did not reappear on the other side.

The pursuing detectives stopped at the wall and looked over. Guy lay at the bottom of a big, deep, square pit which had been made to hold an underground storage tank. He stared up at them, his eyes burning with pain and despair.

Martineau arrived a little behind the others. He looked down into the pit. "Are you all right?" he asked, banally enough.

Guy groaned, and sat up.

Devery had noticed the unnatural angle at which the fallen man's right foot lay. "Don't try to stand up!" he called sharply. "You look as if you've got a broken leg."

Guy moved the leg, and seemed to go sick with pain. Cassidy vaulted over the wall and dropped lightly—for a man of his hefty proportions—into the pit. He knelt and examined the injured limb. He used his big hands as gently as he could, but the examination was not painless. "It's broke, all right," he said with heartless gusto. "He's done all the running he'll do for a long time."

Martineau turned and looked across the road, at No. 49. "All right," he said. "Get him out of there while I go and hear what Miss Grayson has to say."

17.

MARTINEAU'S men hunted around the building site and found a ladder. They used the ladder to get Guy out of the pit without hurting him. They sent for an ambulance. They waited, and at least one of them was near the injured man all the time. Even when he had a broken leg they did not trust him. They had had enough of Guy Rainer.

Martineau talked to Sheila Grayson. She told him the story of her encounter with Guy. "He terrified me," she said.

The detective realized that it was not she who had dialed 999 for the police. "He didn't terrify you at first," he said with a cold smile. "You could have telephoned."

She did not look at him. "I just couldn't bring myself to do it," she said.

"Instead you gave him food. For that you only got a bruised mouth when he turned on you. You've been lucky. You've been twice lucky. He might have injured you seriously."

"I'm sorry," she said. "Will I be in trouble for not calling the police?"

He smiled less coldly. "You've been a foolish girl, but I daresay we can find it in our hearts to let you off."

"That's big of you," said a new voice. They turned and saw that Patricia had come round the side of the house. She also was wearing dressing gown and slippers, but her red hair had been made tidy. She looked fit and fresh and very beautiful. Her glance was contemptuous as she looked at her sister.

"I see you've caught him," she said to Martineau. "Is he badly hurt?"

"Broken leg. Simple fracture, I think."

Her eyes were defiant, as if she expected criticism which she did not intend to accept. "It had to be done," she said. "I wasn't going to stand there and watch him pinch my car. I don't owe *him* anything."

Sheila turned horrified eyes upon her. "*You* phoned the police!"

"Of course I did. What about it?"

"We were on our way, in any case," said Martineau quickly. "The phone call made no difference."

But Sheila was looking at her sister. "Oh, Pat!" she said.

Pat boldly met her glance. "Don't be a damn fool all your life," she said. "What can Guy bring you but grief? I did the right thing, and you know it."

Sheila did not answer. Pat looked at Martineau and shrugged. "I'm going to make some coffee," she said. "Could you do with a drink, Mr. Martineau?"

"Thank you, but I don't believe I shall have time," the policeman replied. "There is still a lot to do."

Pat nodded and turned away. She went indoors. Martineau said to Sheila: "I'm sorry. But your sister is right, you know."

"Oh, I suppose so," the girl admitted. "But I don't know how she could do it."

The ambulance arrived. Rainer was put on to a stretcher and lifted into it. Sheila went across the road to him. "I'm sorry, Guy," she said.

"I hope I never see you again," he replied. "You and your sister are bad luck to me."

"It was all your own fault," she persisted.

"Oh, go to hell," he said, putting his head down on the stretcher and not looking at her.

Devery closed the doors of the ambulance, and it began to move away. Sheila said: "Pat was right. He's a bad 'un," and then she turned and went home.

Still under escort, Rainer was taken in the ambulance to Farways Gaol. Unless his injury was more serious than it seemed, he would presumably be put in the prison hospital.

Martineau, Devery, Cassidy and Ducklin went to Headquarters. There, among other documents, the chief inspector found P.C. 942 Vincent's report waiting for him. He looked thoughtful when he read about the conversation in the Devonshire Arms. Later, as Vincent had expected, Kegan and Rosa had stayed in the Flying Dutchman until closing time, and then they had gone home together. Martineau read over the first part of the report, and decided that Vincent had not been wasting his time. Kegan and Rosa had been worth watching.

Superintendent Clay was still in his office. He looked tired, but he smiled when Martineau went in.

"Good work," he said. "Rainer is back where he belongs, at last. I was livid when I heard about him slipping you at the mill."

"How is little Miss Kegan?" his subordinate asked.

"Very poorly, but she's getting stronger every minute, and the doctor is cautiously optimistic."

"She'll live, then?"

"Apparently she has a good chance. It was a clean job, by the way. There was no other sort of interference with her. When she comes to, she should be able to tell us who tried to murder her."

"How would it be if we pulled somebody in without waiting for the kid to tell us?"

"It would be fine, if we got the right client and enough evidence to charge him. Do you think you can do it?"

"With a bit of kiddology I might be able to manage it."

"Who's your client?"

"One of two people."

"You don't want to tell me yet, huh? All right, go ahead and I'll wait to know."

"I'd like to take Albert Vizard with me."

Clay frowned. "M'm. I don't know."

"He's no Guy Rainer. I'll bring him back safe if not sound."

"You'd better. But why can't everything be done here, in the usual manner?"

"As I see it, I may be able to do it better elsewhere."

"All right, have it your own way."

"Thank you, sir," said Martineau. He went out then to make his own arrangements. He also visited the police library to confirm a point of criminal law.

It was half-past nine when Martineau entered Markham's Mill for the second time that morning. On this occasion he was accompanied by Devery, Sergeant Bird the photographic and fingerprint expert, the mill manager and the office manager. Albert Vizard was sitting in a police car in Eden Street, with Detective Constable Cassidy and a police driver. Cassidy had been well briefed concerning his duties that morning.

Martineau began by asking questions in the warehouse.

"Was it you who locked up this place on Friday afternoon?" he asked.

"Yes, I always go round myself to see that all is secure," said the mill manager, whose name was Bailey.

"What time did you get away?"

"Oh, happen half-past four."

"What was the procedure? Did you use the lift?"

"The hoist, we call it. Yes, I did. I went up to the twisting hole, which is on the top floor. I worked my way down floor by floor to the warehouse, seeing that all was in order. I looked round the warehouse and the shed, then I took the hoist to the cellar, and switched off all the lights at the mains, except the lights for the office and the engine room, which have their own main switches. Then I came up those steps, and went out this way."

"You didn't look round the office, then?"

"No. Mr. Bircher looks after the office, that's his responsibility. He has a key to let himself out if I happen to lock him in."

Martineau turned to the office manager, a sharp-faced, high-colored, dapper little man. "What time did you leave, Mr. Bircher?" he asked.

"Five o'clock exactly," came the prompt reply. "I was alone in the office, just squaring up one or two things. I heard Bailey go out and lock the door. I also made sure that it was locked when I went out."

"This is the picture, then," said Martineau. "Tell me if I'm wrong. Most of the workers were out of the place by four o'clock. A few lingered till—what time?"

"Not much later than five past," said Bailey. "I think they'd be all gone by then."

"Right, and at about ten past four you took the hoist to the top floor and began your usual inspection, and you arrived in the hoist in the basement at about half-past."

"Correct."

"You glanced round the basement, turned off the lights, and went home."

"Right."

"And all the time between ten past and half-past four these two doors, the inner and the outer, were open, is that right?"

"They were closed, but not locked."

"Therefore anybody could have walked unnoticed into the warehouse and gone down into the basement."

"No," said Bircher with some emphasis. "We're not as daft as all that. When folk are going out in ones and twos, and there's nobody much about, I always have the inquiry window propped open. Nobody can go in or out without me hearing them. Look, I'll show you."

He led the way to the outer door, and opened and closed it carefully. It had a strong spring which made a rather musical noise, as if some person with no knowledge of the instrument had plucked the strings of a harp. Then he went to the inner door. The inner door squeaked.

"You can bet your bottom dollar nobody came in this way between four and five," he said firmly. "I'd have been wanting to know who it was and what was his business."

"Thank you," said Martineau. "So we've got to find another door which was open. A door which gives access to the basement, through here or some other way."

"There's a door near the engine room which might have been open," said Bailey. "That's Ben Smith's responsibility, not mine."

"Who is Ben Smith?"

"He's the engine tenter. He locks up at his end."

"Show me," said Martineau.

They went down the steps and through the basement, where Bailey switched on the lights, and Martineau was shown the outer door at the head of the short flight of stairs which connected the engine room with the basement.

"This is a *better* way in," he said.

"It is, if Ben didn't have it locked," the manager agreed.

"We'll have to ask him."

"We can soon do that, he's on the phone," said Bircher. "Shall I go and give him a tinkle?"

"I'd be much obliged if you would," the policeman said, but he took the precaution of sending Devery along with Bircher, in order that the truth of the matter might be efficiently ascertained and routine questions asked.

He went with Bailey and Sergeant Bird to look at the engine room and boilerhouse. "This is where Guy Rainer got in," he said when he saw the boilerhouse door. "I'd get a better lock on that if I were you."

Devery and Bircher met him when he returned to the basement. "Ben left at half-past five," the office manager said. "He was messing about with a valve. He didn't lock the door till about a quarter to five. He didn't remember it till then."

Martineau looked at Devery who nodded confirmation. "He saw nobody and heard nothing," the sergeant said.

Martineau nodded. "So we have established that one or two people *could* have entered this place between four o'clock and half-past, without being seen."

"I'm afraid that is so," was Bircher's reluctant admission.

"How long has Jack Kegan worked here?"

"Oh, years, off and on," said Bailey. "He thinks he's made for something better, and he keeps trying other jobs. But he always comes back here. He's a good worker, I'll say that for him."

"Where did he meet that woman of his, Rosa Vizard?"

"Right here in this mill, very likely. She used to work here as a weaver, and she will again as soon as that bairn of hers is old enough to be farmed out to a baby-minder. She likes to have some brass to spend, does Rosa."

"Did her husband ever work here? Albert Vizard."

"No. But we have his sister Bertha. Big Bertha. She's worked here twenty year or more."

"I see," said Martineau. He was looking around the basement. "Could we have more light in here?"

Bailey glanced at the four dusty one-hundred-watt bulbs over-head. "This is all the light there is," he said. "This place doesn't get used a lot."

"Is this the way it would be between four and half-past on Friday afternoon?"

"This is the way it would be," said Bailey.

Martineau moved around, looking into the waste bags, old skeps and weft boxes which were the basement's contents. One skep was full of heavy leather belting, and another contained a tangle of leather straps. On a bench nearby there was a neat and shining pile of steel spindles, and a larger pile of steel-tipped box-wood shuttles. Beyond the bench there was another skep into which a number of oddly shaped sticks had been thrown.

Martineau took a clean handkerchief from his breast pocket. He was stooping to pick up one of the sticks when Bailey stepped forward to prevent him. "Don't go and mucky a nice clean han'ketch," he said. "Here, use a bit of this cotton waste."

Martineau thanked him. Using the cotton waste, he took one of the sticks by the middle of its length and lifted it out of the skep. He felt the weight of it. It was about the size, but not the shape, of a baseball bat. It was rounded for most of its length but had a heavy, squared end. The rounded part was highly polished, the square end was not polished at all.

"This is a picking stick, isn't it?" he asked.

Bailey assured him that it was. "All this stuff is taken from those old looms we just broke up," he said.

Martineau took out his torch and examined the stick more closely. He showed black fingermarks to Bailey.

"Aye," the cotton man said. "The fellows got their hands cov-ered with black oil when they dismantled those looms."

Martineau nodded, and carefully replaced the picking stick in the skep. He stood in thought, half-smiling, obviously pleased about something. Then he moved on, and eventually, inevitably, worked his way round to the hoist shaft. He saw the patch of dried blood where Dessie Kegan's head had lain.

"Somebody gave her a crack on the head and threw her in there," he informed Bailey. "Then you came down in the hoist and covered her up. Nobody thought of looking under there because the hoist hadn't been moved."

"Nobody but Guy Rainer," said Devery.

"Nobody but Guy," his superior agreed. "But for Guy she might have been undiscovered for weeks."

The beam of his torch continued to move about the floor of the shaft. "No sign of the weapon," he said. "Nip down there and have a closer look."

Devery jumped down into the shaft and searched for a few minutes. "Nothing here, sir," he reported eventually. "A nice even film of dust nearly everywhere."

"All right," said Martineau. "Go and get your camera, Sergeant, and we'll have a few pictures."

When photographs had been taken, the chief inspector said: "Now let us get into the fresh air, gentlemen. Into the revealing sunlight. Sergeant Bird, can you and Sergeant Devery bring that basket of picking sticks? I think you know what to look for."

Out in the yard the others stood and watched while Devery and Bird examined the picking sticks. They did not have to wait very long before the expert in fingerprints said: "I think this will be the one, sir."

They stood in a group and peered at the dark stain on the squared end of the stick. "Blood," said Bircher, with a slight shudder.

"I think so," said Bird with satisfaction. "*And* there's a bit of hair stuck to it."

"Take it to your car and dust it for prints," said Martineau. "When you come back, bring your outfit and some forms."

Bird went to his car, and Devery went with him. Martineau said to the others, "Shall we go where we can sit down and have a smoke?"

176

Bircher led the way into his office, where he produced a box of cigarettes and said hospitably: "Help yourself. Firm's property."

They lit up. Martineau inhaled with deep pleasure. "My word, I'm tired," he sighed. Then he said easily, with a slow smile: "When Sergeant Bird comes back I'm going to ask both of you if you'd like to have your fingerprints taken. That isn't because I suspect you of anything at all. Let's say I'm starting a collection. I might have to ask quite a number of people. You'll get yours back later. You can keep 'em for souvenirs."

18.

WHEN Sergeant Bird brought the fingerprint outfit into Bircher's office, he said nothing about fingerprints on the picking stick. Nor did Martineau ask him. That was a matter which would be discussed in private.

Neither of the two managers had any objection to having their "dabs" taken. They watched with interest as Bird expertly did the job. "Take mine as well," said Martineau amiably. "And we might as well have yours, Devery."

That made Devery stare a little, but he made no comment. The prints were taken, and the outfit returned to its case. Martineau gave thanks and good wishes to Messieurs Bailey and Bircher, and left the mill with his men. He went to the car where Albert Vizard sat waiting in the care of Detective Constable Cassidy.

"Now then, Albert," he said briskly. "When we took the stuff out of your pockets yesterday, there was one thing we let you keep. Where is it?"

"I don't know what you're talking about," Vizard replied.

"Your handkerchief, man. Hand it over."

"I haven't got it. I left it in my cell."

"He had it out and wiped his hands with it only a minute or two since," said Cassidy. "He's in a sweat about something."

With that, Vizard sulkily produced the handkerchief. Martineau looked at it, and saw that it was even dirtier than he had thought. "This is one article you didn't throw into the wash on Friday night," he said with satisfaction. "Cassidy, you saw him give this handkerchief to me?"

"I did, sir."

"And you see these marks upon the handkerchief?"

"I do, sir."

"Very well. Take it and put a personal mark of identification upon it."

Cassidy took the handkerchief. His fingers, which had more than once been compared to a bunch of bananas for size, fumbled in his waistcoat pocket and emerged holding a stump of indelible pencil. He wet the end of the pencil with his tongue, and made a tailed cross, a cross like two hockey sticks, on a corner of the handkerchief.

"Thank you, Cassidy," said Martineau, taking the scrap of soiled, off-white cotton. He glanced at Vizard, who was watching him nervously, and said: "Now you know your instructions with regard to this man?"

The Irishman nodded confidently. "I do, sir," he said.

Martineau turned to the two sergeants. "Come on," he said. "We can walk as far as we need to go."

They set off along Eden Street. Bird was still carrying the fingerprint outfit. "There aren't any dabs on the picking stick, sir," he said. "It looks as if somebody has wiped it off with waste."

Martineau opened the handkerchief. "It was wiped off with this, I suspect," he said. "Look at the black oil."

The time was fifteen minutes past ten, and there was nobody in sight in Collier Street as the three men turned the corner. Because it was Sunday, the street was not yet fully awake. But as usual in mild weather, some doors were already wide-open as a sign that the family was at home, out of bed, more or less dressed, and ready to receive neighborly calls. As the policemen walked along, half-dressed children and women with hair not yet combed appeared in doorways to stare after them.

The door of the Kegan-Vizard house was open. Martineau tapped. "Come in," Kegan said.

The family was just finishing breakfast. It appeared to have been a good breakfast, and the coffee smelled good. The baby was sitting in his usual place on the rug, gnawing something which might have been a kidney. Kegan and Rosa were at table. He was in his shirt sleeves and unshaven, but his face and hands were clean, and his dark hair had been combed. She was wearing the house dress which she had been wearing when the police made their first visit to the house two days before. She also was clean, and her glossy hair had been well brushed.

"Any news?" Kegan asked calmly enough, but with that mixture of hope and dread which was now familiar to the detectives.

"We've found a bloodstained weapon," said Martineau, intentionally casual.

"What sort of weapon?" Kegan was white.

"A picking stick."

"Oh, my God! If somebody's hit Dessie with a picking stick, she'll be dead."

"You *could* call it a lethal weapon."

"Where did you find it?"

"Markham's Mill. In the basement."

"Have you searched for Dessie?"

"Yes, we've searched."

"Why can't you find her? Call yourself a bloody police force!"

"Steady! We're doing what we can. Just now, with regard to the picking stick, we're taking fingerprints. We want the prints of everyone who has the slightest connection with Dessie, or with Markham's Mill. Will you volunteer your prints?"

"Why should I? Do you suspect *me*?"

"Not necessarily. You can refuse if you like, but it would look

179

bad. Everyone else seems to be quite willing. See, we've got quite a collection already."

"Oh, all right. But it seems like a waste of time to me. Find Dessie first, then start bothering about who hit her."

"If we find the person who hit her, he can tell us where he put her, can't he?"

The implication in Martineau's words was too much for Kegan. He covered his face with his hands. "She'll be dead. She's dead. My little Dessie!" he sobbed.

Sergeant Bird began to clear a space for his fingerprinting equipment at one side of the table. He inked the black, gleaming pad and ran the roller to and fro. He purposely did not look at anybody. Rosa watched him with a sort of fascination. Kegan still had his face in his hands. Martineau and Devery were covertly observing him and Rosa.

"Now then, Mr. Kegan, I'm ready for you," said Bird. He put down the roller and placed a fingerprint form at the edge of the table.

Kegan removed his hands from his face. He looked at the pad and the form. He got up rather wearily and moved round the table to where Bird stood. The sergeant deftly took his prints, and then completed the form. "Now you, Mrs. Vizard," he said as he put it aside.

Rosa smiled as she got up and moved round the table. It was an indulgent smile. It gave the impression that she thought the policemen were boys playing some boys' game. Bird took her prints. She stood and watched him as he completed the form.

Martineau remarked chattily to Kegan: "These fingerprint forms can be useful in all sorts of ways, you know. We might be able to find the person who sent the decoy letter to Miss Grayson."

Rosa turned and stared at him, and there was panic in her face. Then she moved. She snatched the fingerprint form from Bird's hands and crumpled it in her own. She looked wildly at the fireplace, but there was no fire. She turned to the door, but

Devery blocked the way. She thrust the crumpled form down the front of her dress.

Sergeant Bird did not observe Martineau's cold smile. He was pink with indignation. "Here, give me that form," he demanded.

"No. I won't," Rosa replied. "I've changed my mind."

"That's a woman's privilege," Martineau interposed. "But won't you tell us why?"

"No, I won't."

"Is it because you were the person who wrote the letter to Miss Grayson?"

"No." Her face was a stiff mask of fear.

"Then why is it?" Kegan suddenly shouted. "Give back that form!"

"I won't!" she shouted in reply.

Kegan rounded the table. Her fingers went like talons to his face. He caught both her wrists and pressed her hands together, and held them both in one of his. She kicked his shin, and her head came down as she tried to bite the hand which held hers. He met the head with the heel of his free hand, and sent it back with a jerk. He reached into her dress and got the form, and threw it on the table. Bird picked it up.

"Now then," said Kegan, freeing the girl. "We'll have some explanations."

But the child on the rug had started to cry. Rosa stooped and picked him up, and began to comfort him.

"You're not geting out of it that way," said Kegan. "You're wasting time, and every minute might count." He snatched the child from her, and ran out of the house with him. They saw him go past the window as he went to the house next door. Rosa went to the armchair which faced the window, and sat with a hand pressed to her forehead. The others waited in silence, until Kegan returned without the child.

"Now," he said. "We'll have a few matters cleared up, but first of all, what did you do with Dessie?"

Rosa looked up at him. Her glance flickered to Martineau, and away. "I never touched Dessie. Honest, Jack, I didn't."

"Come on, we aren't being kidded today. Where's the child?"

"I've told you, I don't know."

"*I* know about you. You told the inspector a lie on Friday, and I let you get away with it because I thought you were just avoiding unnecessary questions. It never entered my head that you could have been the one he wanted. You told him you didn't go out between four and half-past, but you did. You went to the shop as soon as I got home from the mill, and you were gone about twenty minutes. You laid in wait for Dessie, didn't you?"

She shook her bowed head. "No," she said. There were tears in her voice, but Martineau, watching her, could see that she was still obdurate and cunning. She was still a long way from the breakdown point.

Kegan seemed to be restraining himself with difficulty. "It's the money you were after," he said through set teeth. "Little Dessie's money, what you thought would come to me. You thought you'd be able to get it off me. You're crazy for money and clothes and a good time, and you always were. You'd do anything for money. You murdered my Dessie for money."

"I didn't, I tell you, I didn't!" she wailed.

Suddenly Kegan took her by the throat. He lifted her out of the chair. Martineau and Devery closed in and broke his hold. She dropped back into the chair. They held him until he became calmer. Then Martineau spoke.

"I think Mr. Kegan isn't far from the truth," he said. "But unfortunately we don't have enough supporting evidence, yet. If we had, we would take you away, Mrs. Vizard."

She sobbed and gasped, and held her tender throat.

"As it is," went on Martineau, "we will have to leave you and proceed with our inquiries."

She looked up. "No!" she cried in terror. "Don't leave me alone with him. You've seen what he'll do. Don't leave me!"

"What else can we do?"

"Take me with you."

"If I do that, you must tell me what you did with Dessie."

"Nothing, I tell you."

"Where is she?" Martineau persisted.

Rosa broke suddenly. "Under the hoist," she said. "Under the hoist at the mill."

Kegan sprang, but Devery held him. He struggled, and then the strength seemed to go out of him. "Did you kill her?" he asked in a curiously dead voice. Rosa wept wildly, nodding and shaking her head violently, without meaning.

"I brought it on myself," said Kegan. "I should never have left Lucy and taken up with a woman like you. I might have known you'd do my daughter harm, sometime. I can see how you planned it. You wrote that letter to get the teacher out of the way. You met Dessie and told her you were taking her to see her Daddy. Dessie would fall for that one, all right. You took her into the cellar at the mill and hit her with a picking stick from one of those old looms we've been breaking up. You knew about those looms, because I'd told you. You killed my Dessie and slung her into the bottom of the hoist and left her. How *could* you do it? My little daughter!"

Martineau looked at Rosa. She was no longer weeping, but staring out of the window in a dazed way. Whether or not she had been listening to Kegan, she was beyond recrimination. Perhaps, now was the time to get the whole truth out of her.

"Mrs. Vizard," he said sharply, and she turned her head to look at him. "You are not obliged to say anything in answer to my questions, but anything you do say will be taken down in writing and may be given in evidence. Do you understand that?"

She neither nodded nor spoke, but her glance flicked away from his. He knew the sign. Her cunning, primitive brain was working again.

Kegan interrupted. "Never mind the questions. What about going to find Dessie?"

Martineau turned his back on Rosa and faced Kegan. He

winked broadly and held his fists in front of him with both thumbs raised. "Let me handle this now, Mr. Kegan," he said sternly.

He saw hope come into the man's face as he turned away and went to the door. He looked out. Near the end of the street a car was waiting. He beckoned, and went back into the house. A few seconds later the car drew up at the door. Out of it stepped Cassidy and Albert Vizard. They both left the car by the same door, because Vizard's wrist was handcuffed to Cassidy's. The Irishman did not need handcuffs to hold such a prisoner. He was merely striving for dramatic effect.

The newcomers entered the house. Rosa's eyes widened when she saw Vizard. Kegan also looked surprised, but after Martineau's warning he remained silent.

"Hello, Rosa," said Vizard, trying to show a brave front. "Don't let 'em kid you. I've told 'em nothing."

"*She's* told us plenty," said Martineau. "We only need to know a very little more." He took Vizard's handkerchief from his pocket, and held it up by two corners. "Dessie's head was battered with a picking stick, and she was thrown under the hoist at the mill. I think the laboratory will be able to produce evidence that the stick was wiped off with this handkerchief, and the handkerchief was found in your pocket."

Vizard showed real alarm. "Is she trying to tell you I did it?" he demanded.

"Didn't you?"

"I did not. If she says I did she's lying. You can't touch me on this."

"Can't I? I'm going to give you an outline of what happened. You saw Rosa meet Dessie on Friday afternoon. Perhaps you were curious, or perhaps you were still interested in your wife and wanted to speak to her. You followed her into the mill. The lights were on in the basement and you were in there with Rosa and the child. You were present when the child was attacked. I'm not saying whether it was you or Rosa who swung that stick, but I think from your attitude that it was Rosa. However, you helped her to hide the body and you destroyed the evidence of fingerprints on the stick. You went out of the place with Rosa and you thought you were sitting pretty. You had her in the hollow of your hand. You could make her go to bed with you, and in the by-and-by when she managed to get her fingers into Kegan's money, you were in a position to collect."

"You can't prove I did anything wrong," said Vizard. "I'm clear on this."

"You think you are. You know a bit of criminal law, but you don't know enough. I know what's on your mind. You were seeking confirmation of it in the public library yesterday afternoon. You didn't find what you sought, but judging by the way you're acting you still think you're right. I guessed what it was, and to be *absolutely* sure I looked it up myself. It goes something like this: *A wife cannot be convicted of being an accessory after the fact of a felony committed by her husband.* You had heard something about that, and you thought it cut both ways. You were quite wrong. Only the wife has that immunity."

Vizard looked sick. "You're wrong," he shouted. "There's such a thing as equality of the sexes."

"There is indeed," Martineau agreed drily. "But some sexes are more equal than others."

Rosa spoke up, and everyone turned to look at her. "Inspector," she queried. "What was that you said about a wife's immunity?"

Martineau told her again. She frowned in concentration, then she said: "He did it. Albert did it. I saw him. I only kept quiet because he said I couldn't give evidence against him, because I was his wife."

Vizard howled with indignation. "It's a lie! I saw her take the kid into the mill, and I followed. I saw her do it. She was like a madwoman. She'd have beaten the poor kid's head to a pulp if I hadn't stopped her."

"That's not true, and you know it," said Rosa with a certain equanimity.

"Dessie will give us the truth of it, when she recovers," said Martineau.

The Vizards, man and wife, stared at him; Albert with new hope, Rosa in sudden dismay. "She's alive, then?" Albert asked.

"She's safe in hospital."

"Is she bad?" Kegan asked.

"Pretty bad, but she should recover."

"Thank God for that. But why on earth didn't you tell me before?"

"Isn't that obvious? I wanted to use you. The police can't put people in fear of immediate death, you know. That's what you did to Mrs. Vizard. It was you who broke her down, and made her admit guilty knowledge."

"And now we've got to wait till Dessie gets better," said Kegan, looking hungrily at Vizard.

"Not necessarily. When Mrs. Vizard left the house just after four on Friday afternoon, what coat was she wearing?"

"She didn't bother with a coat. She went out just as she was."

"You're sure of that?"

"Positive. I remember she slipped out in a hurry."

"She was wearing the dress she's wearing now?"

"Yes."

"If she is the one who struck the blow, there might be specks of blood on the dress. Could I have a look, Mrs. Vizard?"

"No," said Rosa. "I'm not having you breathing all over me."

"Take off the dress, Rosa," said Kegan.

"In front of all these men? I won't!"

"Take it off upstairs, then, and I'll come with you to see you don't set fire to it."

"No. You might try to strangle me again."

"You want the dress, Inspector?"

"Yes, but perhaps I can get it later, at the police station."

"You can have it now," said Kegan. He seized Rosa's wrist

and pulled her out of the chair. He swung her round, and ripped the thin dress down the back. Before she could get away from him he had torn it from top to bottom. He swung her round again, and literally peeled the dress from her. He held the tattered garment at arm's length, proffering it to Martineau. Rosa, who wore pretty underclothes and looked pretty in them, had reeled toward the table. As Martineau reached for the dress she reached for a breadknife. Then several people moved at once. As she turned, holding the knife low, Cassidy lunged across the table, dragging Vizard with him. He laid his right hand on her arm. She whirled and stabbed viciously at the hand, then whirled again to attack Kegan. Devery had moved in, but he could not get at the knife. Kegan jumped back from the knife and the furious woman who held it. He fell into the armchair and put up a slippered foot in defense. She knocked the foot aside, but by that time Devery was behind her. He caught her arms, and while she was held for a moment Kegan sprang up and grasped the wrist of the hand which held the knife. He put on cruel pressure. She spat in his face as she dropped the knife.

Martineau had not moved. Now, he brought out his clean handkerchief and unfolded it. There was a bad wound on the palm of Cassidy's hand, and it was bleeding profusely. The chief inspector crumpled the handkerchief into a ball and closed Cassidy's fist on it. "Hold it till you get to hospital," he said, and then he calmly turned to the window, to inspect the dress.

On the right shoulder and the torn right sleeve he could see tiny spots which looked like blood. "I think that settles it, more or less," he said. "We'll know for sure when it's been to the laboratory." Then to Kegan: "Will you bring a coat or a dressing gown for Mrs. Vizard?"

Kegan went upstairs and returned with a coat and a dress. Rosa sullenly put on the coat, then snatched the dress and put it over her arm.

"That's it, then," said Martineau. "We'd better be going. What will you do about the baby, Mr. Kegan? Can you find some temporary foster parents?"

"Oh, I'll manage."

"Very well," said Martineau. "Come along, Mrs. Vizard. You must go with me to the police station."

"Aye, go on, Rosa," said Kegan. "Go and take your medicine. And pray every night little Dessie lives. If she doesn't live, you'll be an old woman when you come out of Holloway. And I'll still be waiting to make an end of you."

An hour later, Martineau and Devery parted on the steps of Police Headquarters.

"There's gratitude for you," said Martineau. "The super was as crusty as hell about Cassidy's wounded hand. He said it was my fault, because I should have tried to do the job in the approved way at Headquarters."

"Never mind," said Devery kindly. "You're on week-end leave now."

"So I am. I shall just get home in time to have my Sunday dinner and sleep the clock round."

"And then get up to start work on Monday morning."

"And then do that very thing," the chief inspector agreed.

A man, white-faced and agitated, came running across the road. "This is the police station, isn't it?" he demanded, out of breath. "I've been robbed. I've just this minute been robbed. Is either of you men a constable?"

"No," said Martineau blandly.

"Where can I find a constable?"

"You want a detective. In there, sir. Straight through that door. Ask for Chief Superintendent Clay of the C.I.D."

"Chief Superintendent Clay," the man said. He went panting up the steps.

"Now run for your life, boy," said Martineau to Devery.

〉〉〉 If you've enjoyed this book and would like to discover more great vintage crime and thriller titles, as well as the most exciting crime and thriller authors writing today, visit: 〉〉〉

The Murder Room
Where Criminal Minds Meet

themurderroom.com

www.ingramcontent.com/pod-product-compliance
Ingram Content Group UK Ltd.
Pitfield, Milton Keynes, MK11 3LW, UK
UKHW040435280225
455666UK00003B/97